Reason

to

Believe

Steve Kenning

Reason

to

Believe

TIRADORS press
LONDON + BARCELONA

Reason to Believe

Published by TIRADORS press
75, The Exchange Building,
132 Commercial Street
London
E1 6NQ

tiradorspress@btinternet.com

www.tiradorspress.co.uk

ISBN 978-0-9562199-0-9

First Published in Great Britain by TIRADORS press
2009

1

All five women were talking simultaneously, enthusiastically relaying information, thoughts and opinions to anyone listening. Unfortunately, no one was listening to anything anyone else was saying. They were sitting around a heavy, round, polished deep red mahogany table in the vast, family dining room that filled the whole central area of the large apartment that was so big it occupied the whole of the fourth floor of the building found at Caller Balmes, 378. The conversation between the five women had become increasingly animated, although it was nothing more than a diversion, as for nearly an hour they had waited for a visitor. Their agitation had increased proportionally to their growing sense of frustration.

Reason to Believe

The crescendo of high-pitched conversation escalated from something tolerable to a pitch so ear splittingly unbearable that forced one of the five women seated around the table to stop talking and listen. After a few minutes of taking in the assorted verbal garbage to which she had recently been a significant contributor, she slowly stood up and raised her arms.

'Ok! Ok!' she said.

No one took any notice. The woman, blonde, reasonably slim, in her forties and dressed expensively in a black two piece suit, picked up her glass, and rapped it several times on the dark wood, heavily framed, round table.

'Sisters! Sisters! Stop this!' she shouted, barely loud enough to be heard above the chatter. After several seconds these words had an impact. Gradually the other women all stopped talking and looked at her expectantly.

'What Montse?' asked the only one of the five women who was dressed in jeans, fashionably topped off with a light cashmere woollen sweater. She was prettily attractive and just beginning to reveal the facial fissures of a woman in her mid thirties. Montse looked back at her, holding her in a strong eye contact as she sat down slowly before replying.

'Well Christy, I would have thought that was obvious!' she snapped, 'I would prefer we talk to each other and not to ourselves. The question we all want an answer to is 'where is our father?"

Steve Kenning

'It really is very unlike him to get us all together like this in the middle of the afternoon. He knows we are all busy,' replied Christy, the only blonde in the room.

'What's wrong with our usual monthly lunch? Next Wednesday isn't it?' added Vittoria, 'Next week we will also all be at Montses' birthday celebration. Surely, Papa could have waited,' continued the slightly plump woman sitting slightly removed from the others. The lights from the open plan kitchen illuminated her from behind making her appear far bigger in size than she actually was.

'It is strange, I agree Vittoria,' Montse stated before individually addressing the woman sitting next to her, 'Adrianna, what exactly did Papa say to you on the phone when he called. I know he only spoke to you and me, expecting us to arrange this get together. What he said to me was that it was of utmost importance that we all meet. Because of his insistence I had to cancel a really important meeting with a client. As far as I can remember, the only other time he has behaved like that was when Mama died.'

Adrianna had a natural demeanour bordering on the off-handed and, true to course, up to now she had remained outside of this conversation about Papa. She appeared reserved and quiet although transmitting an intelligent and well-groomed aura. She gently adjusted her trendy D+G narrow black-rimmed glasses before carefully positioning herself forward preparing to reply to the question imposed

6

Reason to Believe

on her. She did all this with such poise that she held the attention of the room for a few seconds. She wore a thin red pinstriped shirt with a huge red beaded necklace over some chic red Versace canvas trousers. Adrianna looked expensive but was more economical with her words.

'The same,' was all she said before relaxing back into her seat.

The conversation paused momentarily as was often the case when Adrianna spoke. The others loved her but had often found her deliberately reserved performance intolerable and mostly put on for effect. Few of them dared take her on in case she embarrassed them with a home truth that only Adrianna was callous enough to relay. The only one of the five with the carelessness to speak her mind was Christy, and once again she filled the silence:

'Thank you for that illuminating insight Adrianna, I'm sure that if you care to take the time to remember you may have a little more to say on the matter. After all I would be surprised if you were any less worried about Papa than the rest of us.'

This direct no nonsense approach always worked. Adrianna's cool, sultry demeanour worked a treat in the sophisticated world in which she moved, but it cut no ice at all with her sisters. She looked a little taken aback by Christy's forthright comments but then quickly moved into sister mode.

Steve Kenning

'Well I have to admit that I have been worried about Papa quite a lot since his operation last year. He just doesn't seem to have recovered that well from the general anaesthetic,' Adrianna continued.

'Yes I agree. He has seemed distant and worried,' added Montse, attempting to heal the fractured sisterly atmosphere.

'Maybe he just got scared,' replied Adrianna, 'After all he is very old,' she paused, 'How old is he, eighty-one?'

The large room the sisters were sat in was a relic from a different generation. Gold leaf dominated the cream and green walls. A huge glass chandelier hung centrally above the dining table around which the five sisters were seated. The earlier air of frustration had gone, replaced now by a mood of concern.

Florita the fifth sister, who exhibited no visible family likeness, stood up and walked into the kitchen to refill the jug of water she had picked up from the table. As she re-entered the living room she made a thoughtful comment to the now hushed assembly:

'Perhaps something has happened to him,' she looked at her sisters, standing jug in hand, 'Here we are moaning about him fixing up a meeting that he hasn't turned up to and all along he could be in trouble. After all, he is eighty-one years old. Yes, we know he is fit and quite agile but

Reason to Believe

anything could have happened. Like Montse said, he has never let us down before.'

They looked at each other.

'We have been here for two hours now. For whatever reason Papa called this meeting, I doubt we will know it today. I have to get back to the office, and I am sure you all have important things to do. Later I will contact the hospitals to check if he has had an accident. Can the rest of you call around to try to find him? If anyone finds Papa, please let the rest of us know,' instructed Montse, who as eldest sister, was obviously the leader of this complex group of women.

'I'll leave a note for him to contact us should he return soon,' added Florita.

They all got up to leave agreeing to phone various people over the next few hours in search of their father.

'I do wish Papa would use that mobile phone you bought him Adrianna. Modern technology!' smiled Christy, as they all walked along the long narrow corridor that led from the dining room to the front door of the apartment. Along the corridor on both sides were three large wooden doors.

'It's strange to think that not so long ago we all slept in these rooms,' commented Vittoria wistfully.

'Yes, it seems only yesterday that we would have a pillow fight and Papa would march into the room in his pyjamas and smoking jacket,' Christy said looking into the past, 'Do you remember that red silk smoking jacket?'

Christy laughed and looked at her sisters. They were all nodding in fond remembrance.

'He would walk in and just talk to us, but we just carried on. It was only when Mama came along and berated us that we stopped fighting,' Christy continued.

'Yes, Papa is and always has been such a big softie with us girls. He let us get away with anything,' added Vittoria.

'I really could never understand how different he was in his job. He was the hardest, most well respected finance minister Catalonia ever had, but we never, ever saw that side of him in this building,' said Florita.

'This was his haven, his escape from a world he didn't particularly like. He confided in me once, once when he had drunk a little too much after a particularly hard day in government. I think he had to deal with a lot of knowledge about things he wished he had no knowledge of. He is an honest and honourable man, but not all the other people in government were,' contributed Montse. She looked up at the others. They wanted to know more about this revelation. Montse thought about her words carefully:

'He told me late one night that he hated the double life he was leading. He said that I was his pride and joy,' Montse paused embarrassed.

Reason to Believe

'We all know that,' interjected Christy, 'what else did he say?'

Montse looked at Christy and smiled, grateful for the support, 'He said that people wanted him to behave in different ways and that he was fed up of trying to please everyone by keeping up a façade.'

None of them understood what their Papa had meant by these words but the sisters looked at Montse with expressions of agreement, understanding and tinged with wistfulness for a memory never to be repeated.

All five sisters eased into the old lift. It was ornately decorated with iron work that was typical of the style of elevator found in most of the more exclusive and expensive apartment blocks in this residential area on the foothills of the Collserola Hills which skirt the western edge of Barcelona, holding the city captive as it struggles to move inland away from the Mediterranean Sea. The women all exuded elegance and exclusive breeding. They looked Spanish, and they all had real class, although they each emanated sophistication in very different ways. As they glided out of the lift as only elegant women can, traversing the apartment concourse and moving out onto busy Balmes, they joked with each other as only very close and supportive sisters do. They hugged, said their goodbyes and each headed off in different directions to their own private worlds. Despite the sisterly humour each of them wore an unmistakable look of concern. They were all thinking the same thoughts, 'Where could Papa be?'

Reason to Believe

2

The city was breathing freely this sunny morning, easily coping with the growing volume of people and cars in its streets on this mid winter day. November was a good month to get around the narrow streets and alleyways of the old city, the Ciutat Vella. There were few tourists and the weather was mild. These particular factors combined made a visit to the heart of the city a real pleasure. It was siesta time, although few people took a siesta in these modern days of air conditioning and global business, a real life situation that made it even easier to get around the streets. It was only the insides of the multitude of bars and restaurants that could be described as crowded.

The sky was crystal blue high up above the city and although the sun was brilliant it was having little impact on the temperature down at ground level in the dark, narrow alleyways. It was chilly on the streets. Such a condition didn't concern Albert Roig, he was pleased to be in the old city and he knew that he had a good few hours ahead of him to make the most of this mediaeval treasure. His next commitment was a meeting at five that afternoon, which meant that for now he could take his time, meet his father in law and then perhaps enjoy a lunch in one of the little bars he loved in the old city. This was the Barcelona he adored To Albert there was no other place on earth that could match the history, the aromas, the character, and th claustrophobia of this special place. Most of his time an life was spent these days shared between the refined world of the Passeig de Gracia and the western suburbs of the city. He worked on Caller Diputacio, just off Passeig de Gracia, and he lived in opulent Sant Gervasi in the eastern suburbs. His work and social life revolved around these areas albeit with a lifetime commitment to a fortnightly visit over to Les Corts to watch his beloved Barça play.

Albert had three loves: his lovely wife and family, F.C Barcelona and the old city of Barcelona. However, if he had to choose between them, Albert would, without a doubt, admit that his heart belonged to the Ciutat Vella. He loved his family and would die for them, F.C. Barcelona was in his Catalan blood, but he felt that the Ciutat Vella was centred in his soul. The area was special to him as it had been home

Reason to Believe

to his grandfather who had delighted in revealing its history and delights to him time and time again when he had been nothing more than a young boy. His views on life, moral standards and ethical stances developed hand in hand with his grandfathers' views as they wandered enthralled amidst the entrancing streets of the old city. Albert was a romantic and bore a great love of history. In his mind, if he were being totally honest, he would reveal that there was no better place to spend time other than in the streets of the old city. He had always wanted to live in this part of the city, in particular to emulate his grandfather, but, despite his heart felt views, he had eventually agreed with his wife Montse's arguments that it was important to live near family and close to good schools, and anyway, in her mind the old city was still a dangerous and undesirable place.

There was a spring in his step as he strolled down Caller Princesca recalling being a young boy exploring these alleyways safe, holding his grandfathers hand. He remembered he excitement of being led from alley to alley by his grandfather who always, on every corner, took time to fill the young boys head with the marvellous history of each and every building that grabbed their fascination. Within seconds, in this retro trance, he realised he had turned onto the oldest street in the city, Caller Montcada.

Albert took a moment to enjoy the vista of the medieval architecture that surrounded him and was happy to allow

15

the stains of hundreds of years of history to wash over him. He stood on the corner of Montcada and Calle de la Barro de Ferro and stared at the angled end of the building that rose up in front of him. The huge stone blocks that made up its walls filled his vista and as his eyes focused on them, he wondered about just what lay behind the closed wooden doors that stood on the first floor. His mind raced into the past and he started to imagine the history of the building and watched it unfold inside his head. He marvelled at the quality of the architecture and the building work. The craft of the stonemason, who had worked with, by today's standards, limited tools, always amazed him when he looked at the grand old buildings of this street. You rarely saw craftsmanship like this in modern buildings he mused. Albert strolled on without looking at where he was walking but instead analysed the shapes and features of the ancient buildings, many of which in past centuries had been palaces lived in by wealthy merchants. He was heading for the building that lay just past the Museu de Textil. This particular building was a hidden gem, few people realised that it was actually the Palau dels Marquesos de Llio. The Palace had been constructed, as were most of the others along this street, in the 13th Century, and although it had been greatly modified over the years, it had retained an atmosphere of medieval decadence about it. As he stood outside the building Albert's heart raced with expectation as

Reason to Believe

the pleasure of the known architectural delights that lay inside the building excited him. The words of his grandfather came rushing back into his head:

'The style of architecture along this street is mainly Gothic. Each palace has an attractive central courtyard surrounded by a main stairwell. This beautiful street dates back to 1148 when Guillem de Montcada gave land to the city.'

Albert looked to his left along the street and enjoyed the gargoyles hanging from the rooftops of some of the buildings. He remembered the phrase his grandfather used to describe them, 'Grandma and her sisters at a family gathering.'

Even as a young boy Albert knew that his grandfather was not being rude about the wife whom he loved dearly. He was simply providing an exaggerated picture of the five loud sisters that dominated his grandson's life. Albert smiled as the memories filled his mind.

For several moments he was lost in his dreams, then unexpectedly he was pulled sharply back into the moment when a familiar voice rang in his ears.

'Albert! Albert! Here! Help me.'

The voice calling out his name took Albert by surprise. He immediately turned from examining the exterior of the palace and looked towards the source of the voice. He couldn't place its owner from the voice alone and he was keen to see who it was. Albert looked around at the crowded street, although it was teeming with people he searched for a familiar face. His eyes roamed from person to person before automatically locking on directly to the figure of Senor Tomeu Ribas Moncada, who had already spotted him and was slowly moving towards him.

'Senor Moncada,' shouted out Albert as he tried to recover his composure by taking a couple of strong steps towards the old man. Senor Moncada was an old man and quite frail on his feet. He reached out his hands to help his father-in-law steady himself.

The old man hated being exposed to such a patronising attitude.

'Pah! I would normally be OK but this pulled muscle in my calf is slowing me down. It is very sore and it restricts my movement,' gestured the old man towards his lower right leg.

The two men greeted each other and moved off towards the large wooden door that formed an entrance to the Palace.

'Tell me how have you been Albert?' asked the old man. He looked sincere, although Albert could never tell the real emotions that lay behind the wily political front exhibited perpetually by Senor Moncada. He was a very experienced and shrewd politician. Albert had decided long ago to simply be himself and to tell the truth at all times when in

Reason to Believe

the presence of the old man. He realised that with a man of such experience of life and of the deceit and intrigue of politics, he could never better the man in mind or word games.

'I am fine Senor,' he replied.

'And the Company?' rapidly enquired Senor Moncada.

Albert was a partner of a significant law firm in the city. He was very aware that through his numerous contacts, having once been a senior legal figure in the city, Senor Moncada knew the economic state of his business better than he did.

'Extremely good at the moment, we have a great deal of new business,' he confirmed.

'I had heard that things were going well for you,' added the old man.

As the two men stood outside the Palace talking, they presented a starkly contrasting picture to the casual observer. Albert was tall, dark and urbane, dressed expensively to look like any successful solicitor should look. The old man in contrast wore a green/brown tweed suit that looked as if it had been expensive ten years ago. His grey hair was thin and he wore an old fashioned moustache that thickly covered the area between his mouth and nose but stretched no further.

Senor Moncada gripped Albert's elbow with his left hand, partly to steady himself but also, after a lifetime in politics, he used it as a technique of control to give Albert a clear indication of who was in charge, an action that was hard to relinquish.

'Shall we go inside?' The old man asked as he looked towards the Palace.

Albert said nothing but simply signalled with his raised eyebrows that he was happy to comply with this request. The huge wooden doors that formed the main entrance to the impressive building were already open and the two men stepped inside into an inner courtyard that was immense. Much of it was occupied by a successful café that was reasonably busy on this particular day. They skirted around the edge of this and headed towards the more private large stone staircase that rose up into the main body of the building. As they did so, Albert's vision was captured by the splendour of the courtyard stonework. The merchant that built this place must have been extremely wealthy as the blocks of stone that formed the walls of the large courtyard were not uniform but shaped in a range of unusual angles to create a magical landscape of stone. The two men strode across the courtyard and started to climb the wide, imposing staircase. As they reached the top, they paused for the old man to get his breath. From the moment they entered the building Albert had been entranced by the stonework of the ancient building. He wasn't paying any attention to the old man.

Reason to Believe

'I suppose you want to know why I wanted to meet you?' asked Senor Moncada.

Albert didn't register. He hadn't heard what his father-in-law had said. He sensed though that the old man was speaking to him. He looked at him blankly.

'I suppose you want to know why I wanted to meet you?' repeated Senor Moncada.

Albert was surprised by these words as his only thoughts over the past few minutes had been centred on the beautiful architecture of the building.

'Well,' he hesitated, 'Yes. I did wonder,' replied Albert.
The old man looked at Albert. He held him in his eyes before looking away and strolling around his stationary son-in-law. Albert noticed his intense, strained expression. He sensed by the mood of Senor Moncada that the old man was about to tell him something that was of great importance. He decided to listen carefully.

The words didn't flow immediately. Albert stared at his father-in-law expectantly but instead of revealing some deep, intimate thoughts, he just shuffled his feet for a few minutes staring at the stone floor. After several minutes, in his own time, he lifted his head and looked Albert in the eyes.

'I was going to tell the girls, my daughters. I even arranged a meeting with them. Did Montse not tell you?' asked Senor Moncada with a hint of disappointment in his voice. Albert didn't fully understand the old man's train of words, but he went along with the tone of the conversation.

'Yes, she told me that all the sisters were meeting you for a special meeting today at two. She was quite excited,' answered Albert precisely.

Senor Moncada glanced at his watch then looked at Albert with a frown on his face.

'Hmmm. It's two thirty now. I am afraid I have let them down. They will be worried about me,' he thought openly, 'I never let them down,' confided the old man forlornly.

Albert looked at the man he thought he had known quite well for the past fourteen years or more. He studied his father-in-law carefully as the old man shuffled around preoccupied on the stone flagstones. He had always liked his father-in-law, and had always held him in the greatest regard. It was a new experience to see him troubled. Albert was interested in why this might be and wanted to know more.

'Why are you here then? It is obviously making you sad,' questioned an interested Albert probing to get to the bottom of Senor Moncada's concerns.

He stopped shuffling and looked again deep into Albert's eyes. He held his son-in-law firmly in his gaze as he told him how it was.

'I really did not want to let them down, but an hour ago I decided that I couldn't tell them what I needed to tell you. I

Reason to Believe

had to tell you and I was only going to tell them so they would support you. In the end I just had a gut feeling that it would be wrong. I decided that to tell only you, was the best bet. It had to be you that I told. I decided then and there that it was only you that I could tell. You may think this strange, but I was sitting having my morning coffee at the Café Music on Balmes when I had a very clear vision of what I had to do.'

'What do you mean you had a 'vision',' Albert asked, 'What kind of vision.'

'Well,' he paused, 'I've been having strange visions for some time. Since my operation I suppose last year. They scared me at first. They were so vivid and realistic. Also, they always happen when I am wide-awake,' continued the old man.

'What do you see?' asked an interested Albert.

Senor Moncada appeared reluctant to press on with his revelation. It took him a little while before he continued.

'In the vision I am always part of the action. It is very real, but it is always in the future.'

'How do you know?'

The old man smiled to himself before quickly reliving an experience.

'In one of the visions I looked at the newspaper I had in my hand and it was two weeks ahead of the real date,' said Senor Moncada.

Steve Kenning

'Anyway, these visions are very real and the things I see do actually happen unless I, of course, choose to change things,' he continued.

'How do you know?' repeated a slightly disbelieving Albert.

'Sometimes the vision is about something small scale and I decide I don't want it to happen. Like, last week I saw Adrianna get her car clamped on Via Augusta in a vision. I saw the time and date on a newspaper in the vision so I just made sure I was there, at the right time on the right day. Then I talked the men who would have clamped the car out of doing it. It was easy.'

'It sounds like an incredible talent,' remarked an amazed Albert. He sensed from the look on Senor Moncada's face that this was no joking matter, so he asked a more serious question.

'How often do you get these visions?'

Senor Moncada was now in full flow.

'I get two or three a day. But I have no choice about what I see and mostly they are unpleasant. I had a vision this morning that made it imperative that I did not meet the girls and tell them the things I had originally intended. That would have been a disaster,' he paused, 'The same vision made it very obvious that I had to see you Albert. I am grateful that you could see me at such short notice. This is extremely important,' revealed the old man grasping

Reason to Believe

Albert's arm. Albert looked at his father-in-law and couldn't help but notice the intense look in his eyes.

Albert was a little taken aback by his father in laws intensity and by the expectation of what he was about to be told. He composed himself before replying, 'Why didn't you tell the girls that you were not going to make the meeting?'

'I had little time and I was unsettled by changing the path of action away from my vision. I couldn't risk them finding out. Also, I have been too busy thinking about what I need to tell you. I discovered yesterday that there is no time to lose. I needed to take action today. Telling the girls was going to be my only hope of doing anything significant I had thought, but then my vision presented me with a more tangible alternative. It presented me with you. You, Albert, fit the requirements perfectly,' said Senor Moncada with passion.

'What requirements?' asked Albert a little unnerved.

The old man stepped forward and held Albert's right arm with his two hands. His face moved within a few inches of Albert's.

'You are the only person I know who is truly totally honest and who is also undoubtedly pure of soul.'

Albert was stunned.

3

It was developing into one of those days when every single thing was seemingly conspiring to frustrate and annoy. Montse was intensely concerned by her Papa's failure to show for an appointment he had purposefully arranged, as she had never known him to be even late for a meeting before, and now, on top of this worry, as she was half way across the pelican crossing, she found herself being harassed by the beeping, flashing green figure perched high up on the traffic light that forced her to change from a stroll to a run in order to avoid the oncoming traffic. To pour oil onto her rapidly developing incendiary mood, the mobile in her handbag rang even though she was still some way from the safety of the pavement. She couldn't ignore it, as it could be Papa.

Reason to Believe

'Shit! Shit! Shit!' she forcibly voiced before realising that she wasn't alone.

'Oh I'm sorry, please excuse my language,' she hurriedly apologised, as an elderly lady walking in front of her turned and gave her a disapproving stare. Montse hurried to the pavement, narrowly avoiding a motor scooter that had been a little too quick off the mark. She stood still and fumbled for her mobile in her stylish black leather bag. Montse had a weakness for handbags and shoes. Most of her handbags came from a wonderfully expensive shop on Via Augusta. She occasionally tolerated handbags from other shops although the store on Via Augusta was unquestionably her favourite.

'Hello, who is it?' she asked into the mobile, but then immediately felt stupid as the name Vittoria flashed on the small screen of her phone.

'Vittoria! How are you, we haven't spoken for at least ten minutes,' she said with a touch of annoyance in her voice. Then she realised that her sister might have useful information about Papa and immediately changed her tone of voice.

'Have you any news of Papa?'

There was a short silence from the person on the other end of the mobile.

'Vittoria! Are you there?' Montse asked urgently before looking at the screen to see if she had been cut off from her sister. When she put the phone back to her ear all she could hear was the sound of someone sobbing.

'Vittoria! Speak to me. Is that you? What is wrong?'

'Montse, I think Papa knows about me and Jorge,' spluttered her sobbing sister.

'What about you and Jorge?' enquired Montse, confused at this latest interruption to her busy day.

'I think that was what the meeting was going to be about,' howled Vittoria.

Montse was anything but sentimental. Albert loved her for many reasons although sentimentality was not one of them. She knew he had been initially attracted by her strong and determined nature. He loved the fact that she could handle any situation and was a formidable woman in a man's world. She didn't do tears easily.

'Vittoria! I am not going to talk over the phone to a gibbering idiot. Listen! Where are you now?' she asked. She was a busy woman with a senior management role in a major world wide pharmaceutical company, trying to get to an important meeting, however, her mantra was that her family always came first and she lived by it.

'I'm standing outside Plaça Molina metro station,' burbled Vittoria.

'I'm not far away. Wait exactly where you are. No, I know, sit down. There is a café near the entrance to the metro. Get yourself a coffee or something stronger. I'll be

Reason to Believe

only a few minutes,' instructed Montse in a voice tinged with both frustration at Vittoria's pathetic approach to life and with care for her little sister.

Montse was a ten-minute walk away from Plaça Molina. That was where she had just come from. She couldn't face the walk back. It would be much quicker to get a taxi. As quickly as she had decided, she looked along the busy road and immediately saw an available taxi. She hailed it and within seconds was on her way to support her sister.

Vittoria Ribes Moncada was thirty-five years old. It was evident on her face that life was turning out to be not quite as she had expected. The lines beginning to take hold on her plumpish skin were of anguish and disappointment rather than of happiness and joy. She, like the other Moncada girls, was a scientist. However her forte was Chemistry, all the others were physicists. Despite her excellence in her field she had little idea about the chemistry between people. Her life was riddled with failed relationships, mainly due to her inability to choose the right type of man. She was a romantic, a lover of the arts, yet she was always attracted to rational, hard-nosed scientists. No man had ever treated her badly, she was a far too strong and sophisticated woman for that to happen, but they all quickly grew tired of her prissiness and her idealistic romanticism. As a result she always became depressed and subsequently always put on

29

weight. Jorge was her second husband, he had been recommended by her father at a point when she was in one of her deepest depressions. At first life with Jorge had been good. Jorge and Vittoria had even started talking about having the child she dearly wanted. But then six months ago the weight started to pile on and her sisters knew something was wrong.

Reason to Believe

4

As the two men rested at the top of the square, stone balcony inside the courtyard of the Palau dels Marquesos de Llio that sat astride the top of the great stone staircase, they were faced by a high set of dark wood double doors. Senor Moncada reached forward and gently pushed the handle to one of them. As the huge door swung open the two visually contrasting men moved inside the building into a lucidly grand room. Its atmosphere was imposing, undoubtedly a result of the preponderance of wooden decoration and heavy dark wood furniture. The floor was made up of large finely polished marble stones of a wide range of matching but assorted colours. Two walls were lined with books, ancient books.

Steve Kenning

Albert closed the huge doors behind him as he followed his father-in-law into the room. The hubbub of people downstairs in the café was now barely audible and Albert sensed that by crossing the threshold into this imposing room it was almost as if they had entered another dimension. The aura that enveloped them was of a different age that reflected an astoundingly real normality that was far removed from the 21st Century. Albert was at a loss to create a logical explanation in his brain for the origin or reason for the feeling that tingled his senses. His ears buzzed, his hands and feet throbbed and his eyes saw everything with a golden glow. This was a new experience for him but one similar to those he had imagined long ago when his grandfathers words had taken his seeing mind deep into the history of the Ciutat Vella. Albert's jaw hung open. He felt as if he had stepped backwards in time several centuries. Senor Moncada could see the wonderment on Albert's face. The old man sensed that his son-in-law's expression was one of great interest, amazement and some confusion. He attempted to help Albert understand.

'Yes, it is a very different kind of place here. But don't get too caught up in it just yet, as it gets even more magical. Follow me,' he said as he grabbed hold of Albert's right arm and guided him to the far side of the room. Senor Moncada deliberately stood with his back to a wall covered with bookshelves before carefully looking around, keeping a clear

Reason to Believe

eye on the entrance to the room. After a few minutes of careful surveillance, with his back still against the wall he reached out with his right hand and connected with something on the stonewall. Instantly, the floor beneath them dropped smoothly and quickly carrying them both well below the level of the room. Albert was so surprised he didn't notice anything until they had stopped moving. All he had felt was the iron grip his father in law held his elbow with. The floor had fallen away beneath them quickly but stopped a few seconds later with a cushioned impact. As the two men stood statuesque trying to let their senses regain some sort of understanding, a huge slab of stone glided into place above their heads sealing off the place from where they had come.

'Huhh! What happened?' uttered Albert belatedly, relaying the shock of finding himself in an unexpectedly different environment. He was marginally comforted by the physical contact with his father-in-law, although he could see absolutely nothing in the darkness.

Senor Moncada still had a firm grip on his arm.

'Don't worry Albert. I am sorry to surprise you but I thought you would enjoy the experience,' comforted Senor Moncada mischievously, 'Now look!'

At that moment lights came on in the room. Albert was stunned. There were decorative, ornate, gold plated lights placed on all the walls illuminating a stone floor covered in a huge gold and red woven Persian carpet. It was an average size room for a Palace, probably once a special meeting room. It was a room that glistened and emanated an aura that Albert was immediately aware of but just couldn't explain. As he stepped away from his father-in-law his senses took in everything they could about his new surroundings but he was troubled by his lack of understanding and awareness of this new environment. What was it he felt?

He moved around the room. The touch of the stonewalls felt special, although they looked exactly like standard stone blocks painted gold. At particular intervals there were floor to ceiling swathes of red velvet curtains and the occasional gold inlaid chair with red cushions. There was nothing else in the room, not even a door. The way they had come in was the only apparent entrance, although Albert had by now lost any idea of where that had been.

Albert sensed that there was something else in the room, an unusual, indescribable presence and a strange aroma. Whatever it was, it was something that Albert just could not understand. He could feel the presence of someone or something else in the room with them, although, as far as he could see, the only other person in the room was his father-in-law. Albert's brain was working overtime. After several minutes he had sifted through his memory banks to no avail, instead he had decided that the presence he felt

Reason to Believe

was unique. Perhaps he couldn't place it because he had never felt such a feeling before. It was as if he was in the presence of royalty or something more divine. Whatever it was, he felt good, the presence made Albert feel special.

'What do you feel?' asked Senor Moncada.

Albert was unsure. He thought carefully about his answer to the question before responding.

'I am not sure. I really can't say I have ever felt this kind of atmosphere before. I feel there is almost a goodness, a holiness emanating from this room. I can't decide what it is.'

Senor Moncada smiled.

'You are feeling what I have felt for the past sixty years or more. A feeling that is so good and so right that you cannot possibly question it. A feeling that drives your life, your morals and your values. It is a feeling that makes you feel that you are leading the right life. It is this feeling that has driven me to achieve what I have achieved in my life. It has been my moral compass.'

'So what is it?' questioned Albert, 'I feel that you may be right Senor, but where is it coming from?'

The old man stepped over to Albert and again gently held onto his right arm. He led him over to one of the walls of the square room.

'Look at the wall, but please don't be scared.'

Albert looked at the plain, medieval stonewall.

Steve Kenning

'I don't see anything,' he said with a tinge of frustrated expectation in his voice.

'Stare at the centre of the wall directly in front of you, look carefully as I turn off the lights,' added Senor Moncada.

The lights of the room were turned off and immediately Albert's mouth opened, then his jaw dropped further and further. He was speechless.

Albert just stared in silence at the wall in front of him for several minutes unable to speak or move. His mind was attempting to provide a rational explanation for what he was seeing. In front of him was the wall. It was made up of numerous large, smooth edged, stone blocks. Expert craftsmanship. But illuminated somehow within the stone blocks was a spherical gold object with a cross on its top-side that appeared to be gently hovering in a space that didn't exist. The vision glowed lucidly.

Albert stared at the vision compulsively. Eventually he stepped back having regained a little composure.

'How is that being projected on that wall? It looks like a projection in the wall. Is there a glass front to the stone?' he asked actively trying to find an answer to his own question. His hands ran all over the wall. It felt like rugged stone.

'I can feel a power source. It's motorised isn't it? I can't see a camera anywhere. It's a really clever trick,' was all he could muster to say in response to this unexplainable sight.

Reason to Believe

Senor Moncada calmly and slowly walked over to Albert's side and shared with him the unusual vision that illuminated the stonewall in front of them.

'That is no trick Albert. That is the source of the feeling that emanates into this room. It was set back into that wall, behind the outer stone blocks sometime around 1930. It is the Millenarian Globus Cruciger.'

'The what?'

Senor Moncada sighed. The look on his face was one of resignation.

'I once vowed that I would never tell anyone this secret. There are only six of us left who know about this room and about the orb, the Millenarian Globus Cruciger.'

The old man looked as if he had aged about five years in the past few minutes. He spoke quietly before suddenly staggering backwards.

Albert instantly noticed the stagger and sensed that his father-in-law needed to rest. He rushed over to the wall of the room and grabbed hold of two large cushions before carrying them back to Senor Moncada. He placed both cushions on the floor behind the old man and encouraged him to sit in them. Then he sat on the floor next to his father-in-law. The two men watched the golden orb hover inside the wall. Albert watched and watched. Deep down inside he knew this must be a trick but his mind couldn't offer any kind of solution, so for now he allowed himself to believe in what he was seeing. Perhaps it wasn't a trick. It was the feeling that emanated from the glowing golden object that made him believe that what he could see was for real.

They sat still, entranced, for many minutes until eventually Albert asked the question that had been on his mind ever since they first entered the Palace.

'So Senor Moncada, please try to explain all this to me. You have brought me to this secret place, I think I deserve the full explanation.'

Reason to Believe

5

Florita Ribes Moncada was as unique a human being as one could ever wish to be. She did everything to be different and loved to stand out from the general melee of life. Florita liked everything that was unfashionable and she was completely asexual, happy with men, women or no one. Whenever she could surprise she was happiest, swimming joyously in the attention her behaviour generated. She loved attention but particularly wanted to be noticed. Unfortunately her appearance did not help her needs, as she was square in shape and fairly broad. She wore her hair bleached white but short, which made her noticeable but not immediately attractive. However, despite her quite crude physical appearance, and partly because of her expensive wardrobe, she still managed to look classy and as such attracted her fair share of men and women who desired to be seen with her. Her profession helped, she was a casting director for the Catalonian Film Company with the responsibility for the dubbing of films and radio shows into the Catalan language. Florita was always in demand as she was excellent at her job, leading to a plethora of actors willing to do anything to get a part in any of the productions she managed. As a result she made plenty of money, was given a great amount of attention and had as much sex as she wanted. All this made her an arrogant and unforgiving individual.

Despite her appearances and all her indiscretions, Florita was, of the five sisters, the most politicised. Following her father 's example she had been the first Chairwomen of the young PPC (Parties Popular de Catalunya) before going on to be an elected member of the Catalonian Government. Her indiscretions with various sexual partners filled the Catalan newspapers of Avui and El Periodico regularly, yet her popularity was never damaged. Her father had always been her mentor and her guide, although in recent months she had lost her political way. Things were not going smoothly and she had felt that her political influence was waning. She was convinced it was due to her fathers other interests. She needed to find out what was concerning him because

Reason to Believe

without his guidance she knew she was only half the politician she could be.

Two months ago, by when her father had fully recovered from a major operation six months before and was beginning to perform as his usual self, he had started to talk about some strange apparitions he was having. This strange talk from a man, who was as logical and scientifically minded as they come, made the five sisters suspicious, creating a general feeling amongst them that he was involved in something that he was trying to keep away from his daughters. However, Florita alone felt that there was something more sinister going on. She couldn't accept that her father, a lifelong politician and supporter of the good for the common person, could be involved in any kind of intrigue voluntarily, she believed that he was being coerced, probably by people in the city with other interests. She wanted to know who these people were. As a result she hired Giorgio, an Italian Private Detective who had been based in Barcelona for the past ten years, to follow her father.

Within weeks he had collected an amazing amount of information on the movements of the old man. He informed Florita of which of her sisters her father visited most. She was told of all his political confidantes, but despite all this information she still didn't know why he was behaving so very differently to his normal self. Her private detective had discovered nothing unusual about his general behaviour. The only thing she couldn't understand were his regular visits to the Palau dels Marquesos de Llio on Career Moncada. He visited the building at least twice a week, sometimes more, but the Detective could never establish why. The only other person that her private detective ever saw leaving the building was a Catholic priest. As a result Florita discounted her fathers visits to this place as purely being of some kind of religious significance.

Her fathers' strange behaviour bothered her greatly, but Florita was also extremely distracted in her life and her work by a torrid sexual affair she was having with Mendez Atholl, a senior figure in an opposition political party in the city. He was married and a significant political figure, making it vitally important that their relationship remained undisclosed. Despite her need for attention Florita was always happy to keep her sexual partners secret.

Florita and Mendez were a secret couple. He was a commanding politician in Parliament but had little physical presence as a personality around the city. His unremarkable appearance and his natural demeanour, abhorrent to ordinary people, gave of a kind of slyness found only in politicians, and made him totally unattractive to the majority. Florita respected Mendez and, foolishly, trusted him, and so, during this relationship she disclosed her recent concerns about her father. Mendez immediately seized on the potential political capital of this information

Reason to Believe

and informed Florita, quite callously and without any concern for her that he considered her fathers actions tenable as he could be seen to be giving tacit support to the more religious Christian Social People's Party of Catalonia (CSPPC) as he was getting older and closer to death. Mendez based his views purely on the fact that many older people offered their support to the religious political parties in the hope that they would benefit in heaven. He ranted on convincingly at Florita that this would harm both his and her political careers if she did not act to put a stop to it. Mendez claimed that her Papa's visits to the priest in the Palau dels Marquesos de Llio would appear to strongly support confirm his view.

A day or so later, following Mendez's outburst, after a period of quiet, solitary reflection Florita had decided to confront her father about his motives. She decided that the end of the forthcoming meeting with her sisters was to be her chosen time. However, when the meeting arrived and as he hadn't appeared she was not only concerned but also quite put out. As Florita left the family apartment on Balmes she decided to personally seek him out and find out what exactly what was going on. She had a deep feeling that he was with his religious friends in the Ciutat Vella. With this determined view in her mind she headed of in that direction.

6

'Alfonso Carboner,' Senor Moncada paused with significant emotional effect on stating this name. Albert stared at the old man blankly.

'It is not a name you will have heard of Albert, that I am sure, but all this is because of him. I have my successful life to thank him for,' he paused and looked forlorn, 'But, now, at this point in time, I wish he had not been born.'

The old man's verbal theatrics left Albert bemused, all he could think and say was, 'Who was this Alfonso Carboner?'

Somewhat deflated, the old man settled down to tell Albert the story of Alfonso Carboner. He made himself

Reason to Believe

comfortable on his cushion, looked at Albert before holding the younger man's forearm. Then he began.

'I know you have been to the wonderful Abbey of Monserrat, the spiritual home of Catalonia as we true Catalonians believe?'

Albert nodded, as virtually every Catalan would.

'Well,' continued the old man, 'Alfonso Carboner was once a middle ranking priest at the Abbey. He wasn't particularly religious and he knew religion wasn't his vocation, but he was from a wealthy family and the expectation was that he would spend at least five years at the Abbey in order to shape his life and his future beliefs.'

Senor Moncada saw the look of little understanding on Albert's face.

'You have to understand that this was an important tradition in the past times, the Spanish middle classes viewed religion as an essential stepping stone to a successful life, despite the ravages of the church in the Civil War,' he paused before continuing along his original path, 'After only three years, when he was about twenty-five Alfonso's beliefs started to take a very significant shape. He was a fully declared and committed Catalan nationalist but for some reason he started to read about the new regime in Germany that was full of exciting and radical new political ideas. As a result, he gradually adhered to the belief that the Germans were laying the basis of the next thousand-year empire. This

45

interest in German politics became almost an obsession with Alfonso, resulting in him forging strong links with churches in Bavaria in Germany in the nineteen thirties which he later visited them often. In 1935 soon after his sixth visit to Germany he decided that life at Montserrat was too restrictive and that the other priests lacked the intelligence or free mindedness to fully understand his views. He was having an increasing number of intense discussions with other priests and, in the end, it was considered by the Abbey's elders that the best course of action would be for him to leave Monserrat. He remained a priest but rented this particular palace from one of his fathers wealthy friends,' Senor Moncada gestured around himself with his hands as he spoke, 'It was available and perfect for Alfonso as it enabled him to spend the next four years here learning, researching and developing a religious movement, the Utilitarian Dulcinian Creed,' Senor Moncada paused.

The old man suddenly looked concerned and stood up from his seat on his comfortable cushion.

'I need to be quick, we have been here for too long already and you must not be caught here. There are a few of us left who know of the place and it is rarely visited but we cannot take the risk. It would be very dangerous for both you and the future of mankind if we are found out.'

Reason to Believe

Albert laughed as he was not quite on the same wavelength as the old man, 'The future of mankind? What are you talking about Senor Moncada?'

This comment stopped Senor Moncada instantly. He focussed intently on Albert. His eyes connected with those of his son-in-laws at close range. Albert could see the fear in them and he became immediately respectful of his father in laws mood. As he stared into the old mans eyes he also thought he saw a little hope.

The two men stared at each other for a while reading each other's thoughts, then the old man spoke.

'You are the one person that I know that can save the lives of thousands, perhaps millions of people. There may be others, but as I told you, I have seen the future. I have seen the horror of where this lifelong belief of mine will lead us if we do nothing. I have also seen that you can stop it.'

The two men sat in silence for a little while longer.

'Please carry on Senor Moncada,' said Albert after the tense mood between them had calmed. Senor Moncada took the invitation.

'I know all about Alfonso Carboner as I was recruited to the Utilitarian Dulcinian Creed by him in the nineteen fifties. I completely believed in him, in the Creed and in his philosophy right up until I had these visions after my recent operation. I claim over fifty years of belief. Everything we believed in made sense and coupled with the beauty of the

47

orb,' he pointed at the object in the wall, 'With the beauty of the orb, I felt the strength and the righteousness to support my actions.'

He shuffled in his seat, 'The orb is the centre of the belief of the Utilitarian Dulcinian Creed. It was placed in the wall by Alfonso Carboner and was blessed by a senior German Bishop. It will glow and hover for the lifetime of this thousand-year empire, unless the power of the orb is effectively 'turned off' by someone more pure of soul and honest than the person who blessed the orb initially. It cannot be destroyed in any other way. The orb is made of a substance from another world. I have never seen anything like it. The orb is a Christian symbol of authority used throughout Europe since the Middle Ages.'

The old man was in full flow now and he brimmed with the excitement of this revelation. This was undoubtedly the first time Senor Moncada had discussed any of this outside of the Creed.

'It symbolises Christ's dominion over the world, that's the cross and the orb. It also represents each Millenarium, a thousand year empire. The Nazi Party used the terms Drittes Reich, meaning "Third Empire" and Tausendjähriges Reich, "Thousand-Year Empire", to describe the greater German ethnic empire they wished to forge. Alfonso Carboner recognised this as a religious

Reason to Believe

movement and the opportunity to cleanse the world of evil. He wanted to be part of all this,' continued Senor Moncada.

'Please continue,' urged an increasingly fascinated Albert.

'The Third Reich followed The Holy Roman Empire, deemed the First Reich, which had lasted almost a thousand years, from 843 to 1806, hence the Nazi reference to the 1000 year Reich. The Second Reich was the Prussian-ruled monarchy called the German Empire, and the first firmly unified German state, which existed from 1871 until its replacement by the Weimar Republic following the abdication of Kaiser Wilhelm II in 1918 and the abolition of the Empire in the wake of the Treaty of Versailles in 1919. Although this Reich was obviously halted far too early.'

Senor Moncada was getting a little restless, 'We must leave this room. I will tell you more later, although before I finish I must tell you that Alfonso Carboner never supported the genocide of Hitler. He believed in the vision of a holy thousand-year empire. Hitler started this latest millenarium but he became too distracted with power and subsequently lost the religious essence of what he had started. Following Hitler's demise, Alfonso Carboner believed that the orb could be maintained without a ruling power. He had faith that it could change the way people lived. The basic belief of our movement is based on the ancient Dulcian religious movement – which unites people of all religions, including

Muslims, Jews and Christians – which is that the strong and pure will survive. The strong and pure of course refers to those people with strong religious beliefs, the support of God in their lives and who are pure of soul.'

At that point he paused. The old man looked exhausted and the fear had returned to his eyes. Albert hung on to the words he knew would follow.

'Unfortunately, the remaining priests, members of the Dulcinian Utilitarian Creed, including me, have for several years been working on a strategy to ensure that those who don't believe in God, and who are not pure of soul, do not survive. We have in fact been planning our own Armageddon.'

Reason to Believe

7

'Yes, I'm already here, at Passeig del Born. I'm standing outside some kind of creperie. Hurry up it's cold and I'm getting bored. I've been here for over ten minutes now,' grumbled Christy in a cheery voice. For roughly eighty percent of her day-to-day life she was nearly always up-tempo and high octane, as she disliked showing any sign of negativity. The rest of the time she was crashed out. Christy liked to live life to the full and that often involved drink and sometimes soft drugs, which meant that her body couldn't always cope. Time was nothing to her when she was having a good time, although when life was a little more mundane she hated to be kept waiting.

'If you dressed more sensibly you wouldn't be cold, it's even fairly mild for November,' retorted Florita into her mobile. She couldn't see Christy but she recalled that earlier in the day in the apartment on Balmes Christy was clad in jeans and an expensive T-shirt covered only with a loose mohair jumper. Christy had achieved her objective to look good but, in this moment of reflection, Florita considered that a sensible coat would have been the additional accompaniment adopted by most clear thinking people.

'You always think of the moment and never about the future Christy,' scolded Florita, although her own record with relationships hardly put her in the position to offer advice in relation to forward thinking. She added, 'I will be there in two minutes, I'm walking as fast as I can.'

'OK! OK! See you in a minute,' responded Christy, keen to get her chastising, forceful sister off the phone. She put her mobile into her pocket and crossed her arms to hug some warmth into her body. Florita was right in her assumption, she was still only dressed in jeans, T-shirt and skimpy jumper. Christy looked around the busy street lightly jumping up and down on alternate feet to keep warm. Almost instantly, Florita came tumbling around the nearest corner.

Florita, despite her pretty name, was nowhere near as naturally attractive as the slim, alluring, blonde Christy. Who, despite her thirty-five years still received backward glances from many of the younger men she passed in the street. However, Florita looked particularly good today. She

Reason to Believe

always dressed well to make the most of her short, squat figure. A Hugo Boss grey embroidered dress, covered in an exquisite Carmelo black jacket, made her stand out from every other woman on the crowded street. Florita was a couple of years older than Christy, this, plus the fact that she was a significant local political figure, meant she always felt she held the higher ground with her younger, fun loving sister.

Florita spotted her sister and flung herself at her, spreading her arms around Christy in a warm embrace.

'Christy, you may be hard to pin down sometimes but you are always there in a time of need,' announced a smiling Florita.

Christy hugged her sister silently not knowing whether she had just been complimented or otherwise.

'It's lucky I was in La Ribera, Florita. I had to pick up the latest card trick that Julio wanted from the magic shop on Princesca,' said Christy as the women retreated from their welcome hug and stood a little way apart on the busy street.

'Oh, look at this place,' cooed Florita, almost ignoring her sister's words. She looked up and down the wide-open street. At one end she could see the grand ironwork design and imposing structure of the old Born Market, and at the other the enticing intensity of the gothic church of Santa Maria del Mar.

Steve Kenning

'I always want to go inside that church when I see it. It's something about the shape, the small doors and the whole mystery of the building. It just draws you into its history!'

Florita realised she had ignored her sister and tried to make amends, 'Oh, I'm sorry Christy, I didn't mean to ignore you, it's just that I haven't been down here for months,' she oozed. Then she quickly turned off the emotion and returned to the present situation just to show she had been listening earlier.

'So did you get the magician trick for your beautiful little boy?'

'He's hardly little anymore, he's nine years old,' replied Christy. Although she was single she had deliberately had a child without any real knowledge, or later involvement, of the man who was the boys father. She had wanted a child and she had had one.

'You are a great mother, I have to give you that. He always comes first, where is he now? With Aunt Contessa?' asked Florita.

'No. He's at school. I've got until five, then I must collect him,' replied Christy, 'Tell me what you know about Papa?'

'Let me tell you as we walk. We need to go this way I think,' said Florita as she lightly held onto Christy's arm and set off at a quick pace. The two women talked as they walked. They headed along past the old church of Santa

Reason to Believe

Maria del Mar and into Calle Banys Vells, a small alley to the right of the imposing building.

'So you think Papa is illegally helping the Church politicians?' asked Christy.

'I'm not sure. He's so morally right that I can't really believe he would do anything illegal, but he might be trying to help them. What I do know is that he has been very different, very secretive, over the past few months. He has not been the Papa we all know. Also, I know from my colleagues that he spends the vast majority of his time down here in the old city. The Church still own a great amount of property down here, particularly many of the old palace buildings,' explained Florita.

Christy nodded her agreement.

'I don't think Papa would do anything underhand, but have you considered that it may be nothing more than he is just scared of dieing. Maybe he just wants the support of his religion in his final days?' mused Christy. As the two sisters walked along the alley talking, Christy noticed that Florita was increasingly distracted in their conversation, purely because she was looking around at the buildings, searching for something.

'What are you looking for? Is my conversation boring or what?' stated an interested Christy.

Without looking at her sister, Florita provided Christy with a vague reply to her question.

Steve Kenning

'Apparently the Church hid the ownership of many of its buildings during the Franco era. It's impossible to trace which buildings they own, but I am told it is the bigger buildings, the old palaces that are mostly in the ownership of a variety of religious groups.'

'Tell me exactly what we are looking for?' asked Christy, keen to join in the look and find game Florita had started.

'Well apparently it's a palace or a building with only two storeys, which is unusual for this area, that has a fairly new roof. I am told you can see the wooden joists overhanging the stone walls, and the windows on the first floor are heavily barred.'

'Why do we need to find this place?'

'A friend of mine said he saw Papa outside there a week or so ago on two different occasions,' replied Florita.

'I think we are in the wrong place here,' added Christy, 'Here we are behind the palaces on Calle Montcada. I think we need to be on the other side of that street.'

'You could be right,' added Florita, 'Let's cut through this alley.'

The two women soon found themselves jostled by people along the crowded Calle Montcada. The long queue of tourists outside the Picasso Museum left very little room for passers by. Florita and Christy took refuge in the doorway of the Museu Textil I d'Indumentaria before looking up and down the street in search of their evasive building. As they

Reason to Believe

glanced along the street towards Calle Princesca they both simultaneously focussed on a familiar body shape shuffling along the street some seventy metres away. Instantly the two women both prepared to shout out 'Papa' but then simultaneously they drew their words back transfixed. The figure walking alongside their father was also very familiar. Tall, suave and with a dark, full head of hair. Even as they watched this man from behind they still fully recognised him, then both men turned the corner and disappeared along a smaller alley that ran off Calle Montcada.

'Albert! It's Albert!' cried out Christy in astonishment.

Florita was simply staring at the space where the two men had been with her mouth wide open.

'How come Montse had no idea that Albert was meeting Papa? Montse and Albert are really close,' stated an exasperated Christy.

'The perfect married couple, they talk to each other about everything. But you are right, Christy, Montse was as worried about Papa this morning as we were, she couldn't have known that Albert was meeting him,' added Florita, having recovered her usual calm. She then grabbed hold of Christy by the arm and raced along dodging the pedestrians to the point on the street where the men had disappeared.

As they swept quickly round the corner of a small alley, Calle de Cremat Gran I XIC, they were forced to stop suddenly as they saw, just a few yards ahead of them, Albert Roig and Papa slowly walking and talking.

'Wait!' instructed Florita holding out a hand to steady her sister, 'Don't let them see us. I want to know what is going on.'

The sisters drew back slightly and rested close to the wall of the dark narrow alley. By now the two men had crossed over a recently cleared area of land, which had created a welcome wide-open space amidst the dark, dank streets. A small café was busy with people wrapped up in coats and scarves but still willing to enjoy a conversation over a coffee beneath the winter sun. The two women watched Albert and their papa talking. They relaxed a little as it became evident that the two men were so deep in conversation they would not have spotted anything or anyone else.

Reason to Believe

8

'Albert, I want to explain all this to you as simply as I can, but first we must go indoors, in case there are prying ears along this busy street. So, as we walk, instead let me replenish your love of the history of this ancient area,' said Senor Moncada as they stepped outside the building that housed the Textile museum. The two men stood and looked up and down the busy street.

'You probably know all this already, but what the hell, I really enjoy the sound of my own voice,' the old man chuckled to himself for the first time since they had met.

Despite this attempt at humour, Albert still sensed some nervousness in his father-in-law, although he couldn't quite understand why this should be. However, as he was an inherently patient man he decided to stick it out with Senor Moncada to see where the old man was leading him. He played along.

'So tell me Senor, I want to know more about this street in particular. My grandfather told me a great deal but I must have forgotten a lot of it over the years. Refresh my mind!'

The old man looked at Albert, thankful for the opportunity for this diversion from reality.

'As you know Albert this street runs down towards the sea and is full of palaces that were built from the Middle Ages until the 18th century. The architecture is mainly Gothic and the palaces tend to have attractive central courtyards surrounded by a main stairwell.'

Senor Moncada was pleased with his knowledge. Albert tried to look interested but he did know all this. The old man continued to roll out the facts.

'The street dates back to 1148 when Guillem de Montcada ceded the land to the city and this area soon became the centre of commercial life in the Ribera quarter. The finest palace along the street is Palau Berenguer d'Aguilar, which now houses the Picasso Museum and dates from the 13th century. The next two down the street are Palau Castellet and Palau Meca. Just opposite is Palau dels Marquesos de Llio, where we have just been, housing the Textile Museum. Next-door lies Palau Dalmasses, rebuilt in

Reason to Believe

the 17th century. Finally, at number 25, is Palau Cervello-Giudice. Lots of palaces, what a wonderful street!' exhorted Senor Moncada.

'Montcada? Moncada? Is your family name derived from Guillem de Montcada?' queried Albert with genuine interest.

Senor Moncada was enjoying himself now. It was as if his troubled mind had been wiped clean. He smiled at Albert.

'If only. There are the Montcada descendants still in the city. They are extremely rich. You know them, Laurent de Montcada and his sister, Francesca?'

Albert nodded, he did know of them.

'My family, the Moncada's, are from the village of the name near Valencia. Poor peasants the lot of them!' chortled Albert's father-in-law.

Albert looked carefully and deliberately at the man he had admired for as long as he could remember. What he couldn't understand was why he was behaving like this. Senor Moncada was a man who loved talking but who always had something to say. Now though he was talking like a city tour guide and rambling about things he would never normally consider to be a worthwhile use of his words.

The old man moved on. It was as if Senor Moncada sensed Albert's disappointment in him. He stopped speaking mid sentence about another edifice and moved away from where they were standing. He signalled with his eyes and his hand for Albert to follow. They turned right along Calle de Cremat Gran I XIC, a narrow alley that led into a newly opened square. Albert instinctively knew they were walking alongside the rear of the Picasso museum. His attention returned to Senor Moncada as they strolled along, without warning the old man started to reveal his thoughts to his trusted son-in-law. It was as if the words were bursting to get out of his mouth.

'Albert. This is basically a struggle between good and evil.'

Albert was stunned. He stopped momentarily and quizzically looked at his father-in-law.

'I'm sorry sir, but I am a little lost by the train of your conversation. What are you saying? What is a struggle between good and evil? I am really confused by your words Senor Moncada. You need to tell me more. I really do not understand.'

Senor Moncada paused, he turned towards Albert, looked around him furtively, reached out and took Alberts right hand and held it between his hands. Then he whispered, 'I am a Millenarian.'

Albert had no idea what he was talking about.

'I'm sorry Senor, but I still do not understand. What is a Millenarian?' responded a confused Albert.

Reason to Believe

The old man looked at Albert, his face was weary, 'Albert, you need to look into all this for yourself, you must, for only you can resolve this crisis I have helped to create. You must discover as much as you can about millenarianism and what its followers are trying to achieve. I can only tell you so much and help point you in the right direction. Otherwise your purity will be compromised.'

Albert was completely adrift. He was becoming a little annoyed by Senor Moncada and his deliberately mysterious words. His mind was racing, 'What was his father-in-law talking about? Where had all this stuff he was talking about to do with something called Millenarianism come from?'

Albert felt at that moment that Senor Moncada had lost all sense of reality. His father in law seemed confused and was rambling arbitrarily with his words. As he pondered over what Senor Moncada had been saying to him, he suddenly remembered seeing the orb. The feeling of 'goodness' that had come from the orb engulfed him once again, this time purely as a result of his memory. Albert still couldn't find a reason to explain the impact of the orb. His thoughts were unusually indecisive, 'Maybe there was something to all that Senor Moncada was saying. Maybe he should just give the old man more time to fully explain himself?'

As they continued to walk slowly along an alleyway, Albert, deep in thought, lost all sense of where they were.

Steve Kenning

His attitude towards the old man changed and he became fascinated by where their conversation would lead.

'I really need to know more Senor. What else do I need to research?' asked Albert urgently.

'Millenarianism, although I understand it is sometimes also called Millenarism or Millennarism,' said his father-in-law carefully.

'Millenarianism is the belief by a religious, social, or political group or movement in a coming major transformation of society, after which all things will be changed in a positive, or possibly a sometimes negative or ambiguous, direction. My understanding is that it is based on a one thousand year cycle, and this is what we have recently entered.'

Albert had no idea or understanding of what was being said.

'Why am I involved? I have no idea what you are talking about Senor,' spluttered a confused Albert.

Senor Moncada looked forlorn.

'I have not explained things well. You need to find out more about three things: About my Creed, Millenarianism and what exactly is going on in that building over there.'

As the old man spoke he pointed to an unusual looking building.

'Wait here for five minutes. Two people should come out in that time. Wait a few minutes longer and then I will call

Reason to Believe

you in. OK?' questioned Senor Moncada deliberately. He waited for an answer from Albert. The younger man nodded his agreement with his plan. Then the old man strode over to the building and entered it through the large wooden door that opened out onto the alley. Albert was left alone. He felt a little numb and dumbfounded. He hated mystery. He was a lawyer who liked certainty and order.

A few minutes later Albert was running the conversation with Senor Moncada through his head again as he continued to stare at the strange looking building rising up in front of him. The size of it was unusual as it was only two stories high in a district of four or five storey buildings. The roof was new and overhung the walls, but the strangest part of its structure was the heavily barred windows on the second floor. The building was incongruous with the architecture of the area. Albert looked around. He realised they must have passed down Calle dels Flassaders and stopped here along Calle de la Cirera.

'Albert! What are you doing?'

A familiar voice echoed along the tight, narrow alleyway towards him. He looked to his left and saw his sister in laws Florita and Christy rushing towards him.

'Where has Papa gone?' asked Christy.

Albert immediately recovered some composure.

'Into that building.'

Steve Kenning

He pointed.

Christy and Florita followed the direction of his arm.

'It's that building we were looking for,' shouted Christy excitedly.

Florita studied the building in front of them and agreed with her sister, 'Yes, I believe it is.'

Then she turned her attentions on Albert.

'What are you doing with Papa? Didn't Montse tell you we were meeting him today?' stated Florita in an accusatorial tone.

Albert held back his comments for a moment before replying, keen not to antagonise his clearly agitated, potentially volatile sister-in-law.

'Montse said you were all meeting this morning at Balmes, but I didn't know exactly when. I was very surprised when your contacted me, but that wasn't until about 11 a.m. I presumed your meeting had finished. He was lucky to catch me. He insisted we meet in the Ciutat Vella today. He sounded quite desperate,' Albert carefully explained.

Florita had always trusted Albert implicitly. He was an honest a person a you could ever meet. She had known Albert for twenty years and never known him to lie. He was her voice of reason whenever she had a tricky political decision to make and he had never let her down. She looked at him. Florita decided that twenty years of trust was worth

Reason to Believe

savouring. She changed tack and eased her aggressive attitude towards her brother-in-law.

'What did he want?'

'I don't know,' replied Albert, 'He Is just very worried about something. I don't know what or why but I think he is scared of something.'

'Death?' asserted Christy.

'No, I don't think it is that. He doesn't seem like a man preparing to die. I think it is something more,' replied Albert.

'Why did he want to meet you then?' added Christy.

Albert smiled wryly to himself as if unsure as to whether or not to tell the two women. He began gingerly, 'You will find this hard to believe,' he paused, 'He just said that I could save the world! What was even more amusing he emphasised that there was only one person that could - me!'

The two women looked at each other unsure as to how they should react. Standing in front of them was a man that never lied. The sisters were silent for a moment. Then they both came to the same conclusion, virtually at the same time.

'Papa. He must be losing it,' they jointly said using similar words.

Albert said nothing but nodded in silent agreement, slightly relieved that the sisters believed him. The three stood for a moment almost at a loss of what to do next. Christy was the first to get them thinking clearly again.

'Why has Papa gone inside that building?' she asked, 'And what is it? It's a weird building.'

'There are many strange buildings tucked around these streets. That's partly why it is so magical around here. I remember my grandfather pointing this building out to me many years ago. It was built as a storage area for, I think, tobacco, probably in the seventeenth Century. The interesting design was, apparently, quite groundbreaking at the time. The air would flood in from below and the tobacco kept on the first floor was kept dry,' Albert informed precisely. He glanced at the sisters and sensed they didn't want any more of the history lesson. There was a little more to tell however, so he spoke more rapidly.

'Centuries later the building was used by the church as some kind of school for their young priests. I really don't know what it is used for now.'

'Thanks for the history lesson Albert, but all we want to discover is why Papa went in there,' said an irritated Florita.

'That I do not know. He just looked worried and told me to wait here. I think some people will come out soon, he said two people would. It is probably best to keep out of sight,' replied Albert cautiously.

'What?' said a surprised Christy, 'Why is this all so secretive?'

Reason to Believe

'I don't know. But I sense it is,' said Albert, 'Your father is acting like it is a matter of life or death. I decided earlier to just follow his lead and to see where it led to.'

Christy and Florita nodded tacitly their understanding and the three of them retreated a little down the alley into the shelter of a stone doorway. They kept their eyes on the wooden door to the two-storey building that stood twenty metres away.

9

Exhausted, Adrianna hauled herself out of her chic, Danish designed queen sized bed. She adored the black leather headboard that contrasted with the luscious red bed ware that swamped the specially made down filled mattress. She felt much better now. Any contact with her sisters exhausted her, as, in their company, she was simply one of the Moncada girls and couldn't easily settle into her usual and effective cool and aloof persona. Her sisters always probed her, teased her and invariably got under her skin. Today had been like every other meeting since she had left the Balmes home some ten years ago and developed her own personality. It had been tense and tiring. On return from her fathers' apartment earlier in the day she had not

Reason to Believe

only felt tired but also unwell. She had gone straight to bed to regain her strength and her style.

Now Adrianna felt good. She got out of bed and spent twenty minutes in her bathroom rearranging her looks. She had naturally good looks but at thirty-nine she had to spend a little more time filling in the cracks. She re-entered the bedroom and approached the wardrobe. Carefully, she selected black underwear, a black shirt and black jeans. The final touch was her favourite ankle length black boots. She smoothed her clothes down and looked at herself in the full-length mirror that stood prominently just next to the door. She looked good. She approved. She felt good.

She loved her father but she felt nothing for him. Her mother had been the prime parent when she was growing up, her father was always away, always involved in political life. He had led a good life but now he was old and decrepit. Adrianna didn't feel heartless but realistic. Her father could collapse and die at any time. He was old. She couldn't really understand her sisters concern. She certainly wasn't going to waste time looking for him, she felt he was certainly old enough to look after himself. There were many other things to do, most importantly it was late afternoon, the shops were still open, and there were potentially three more hours of shopping. She was ready.

Adrianna put on her best short black denim jacket, had another quick look in the mirror, yeah she still looked good.

Steve Kenning

She moved over towards the door. The phone rang. Adrianna hesitated. Should she just go and leave it or should she answer it? She moved towards the phone and looked at the caller ID. It was Montse. What should she do? It was bound to be a call about Papa. She was annoyed with herself. Why had she looked at the phone? Now she had a real dilemma. The phone continued to ring.

There was only one course of action. Answer the call. Adrianna picked up the receiver.

'What?' she said curtly.

'Charming as ever Adrianna,' replied her sister Montse.

'Listen. I'm about to sit down with your sister Vittoria at the café outside Plaça Molina metro station. She is distraught because she believes her second marriage is breaking down. I have been doing my best to listen to her troubles and to comfort her but you more than anyone else understands that sympathy doesn't come easily with me. Also, Vittoria never really listens to me. I'm just the mother figure. It is you she admires and emulates. She stayed with you for a while the last time this happened didn't she? You both seemed to get on well then. Can you come and talk to her? Give her some advice?' continued Montse in a voice bordering on desperate.

Adrianna paused before replying. Hearing Montse almost begging her for help was a new experience and she quite enjoyed the sensation. Also, she liked Vittoria more

Reason to Believe

than any of her other sisters. Vittoria loved the lifestyle Adrianna led and never judged her. She was the one sister Adrianna would do anything for. The response to Montses' request was easy.

'OK,' she said with reluctance written all over her voice, although this was purely to make Montse feel a little awkward about having asked her for a favour.

'Don't bother if it is going to get in the way of your life,' replied Montse sarcastically. She openly disliked her sister Adrianna'a selfishness.

'No, don't worry I am coming. It is only two streets away. Give me five minutes,' responded Adrianna, resisting the temptation to return a venomous comment.

Within ten minutes the three women were sitting at a table outside the Bar Molina talking and enjoying three beers. Vittoria was laughing and relaxing in the attention her sisters were giving her. Even Adrianna was enjoying this interaction with her two sisters. She had always found Montse too old for her. She was bossy and not interested in her kind of fashion and the other things Adrianna loved. Montse considered Adrianna's life peripheral to reality, almost decadent. Whereas Montse, in Adrianna's eyes was a real scientist concerned with life without frivolity, life where everything is black or white. She admired her elder sister, particularly as Montse always looked very smart and always appeared to be in control, regardless of the situation.

Steve Kenning

Adrianna knew that she would want Montse by her side in any crisis. Her marriage to the equally precise Albert seemed perfect as well.

Vittoria on the other hand was a disaster when it came to love. She was too nice, a terrible judge of character and unable to cope with any unpleasantness. Conflict resolution in the life of Vittoria amounted to sobbing relentlessly with her head under a pillow for several hours simply hoping the original problem would be gone by the time she resurfaced. This type of strategy made her virtually impossible to live with, particularly as her chosen type of partners was often lacking in any kind of empathy. During her last marriage break up she had lived with Adrianna for several months and lost a lot of weight. Buoyed by Adrianna's shopping habit she started to dress well and to feel really good. They had both enjoyed the experience. Their relationship had certainly benefited from this spell together.

As she sipped her beer Montse decided to change the tone of the conversation.

'So Vittoria what do you think? Is Jorge seeing someone else? You say he is spending a lot of time away from home. What's he up to?'

'I don't know. I don't think so. I don't know what to think,' she flustered, 'He just looks worried all the time and he will not speak to me about anything that is on his mind.'

Reason to Believe

Adrianna joined in the conversation, 'How long has this been going on for?'

'Probably six months or more,' replied Vittoria, 'I can't stand it. I don't feel any love or warmth from him and, you know me Adrianna, I need to be loved,' continued Vittoria as tears welled up in her eyes again.

Adrianna put a comforting hand on her sisters' shoulder.

'I think you need to tell him you intend to leave him if things don't change,' suggested Adrianna.

Vittoria looked up at her before bursting into a fully blown sob.

'Come on Vittoria, come now. That is a good suggestion,' added Montse as kindly as she could. She hated weakness in women. All her family were strong women, with the exception of Vittoria.

'I have already said that to him, about three weeks ago. He just acted as if he hadn't heard me. I don't think he has spoken to me directly for over a month,' responded Vittoria still sobbing.

Adrianna and Montse looked at each other as Vittoria sobbed into her hands. Montse held Adrianna in her typically forceful stare until Adrianna was forced reluctantly to look away. She knew Montse was right. Without saying a word about what was needed, the two sisters simply nodded at each other in agreement o the only course of action possible in the circumstances.

Steve Kenning

'OK sister,' started Adrianna, 'You are going to come and stay with me for awhile. Let's see if Jorge misses you then. We will also find out if you miss him a well as visiting shopping heaven. What do you think?' she paused smiling, 'Are you happy about this idea?'

Vittoria stopped sobbing and looked up at Adrianna and her positive, smiling face.

'Oh yes, its just what I need. Thank you Adrianna,' she said with a huge grin spreading across her face.

Adrianna sighed silently before replying positively.

'Come on then, let's go and pick up some of your things from your place. We could also leave Jorge a note. It will be interesting to see his response,' said Adrianna.

The three women paid for their drinks and strolled off towards Vittoria's apartment block. By now it was mid afternoon.

Reason to Believe

10

The wind had suddenly picked up and was gusting fiercely down the narrow alleyways of the old city, the Ciutat Vella. Dust and leaves filled the air. The two sisters, Florita and Christy, were dressed smartly and were trying to appear casually incongruous to any passer-by as they loitered in an ancient doorway accompanied by a suave, dark haired, urbane man who just happened to be their brother-in-law, Albert.

Ten minutes had passed since the old man had disappeared into the strange two-storey building. Nothing else had happened. The occasional person passed quickly by them, sometimes with a wary look in their eyes, but mostly nonchalantly and without interest, whichever approach appeared to be dependent on whether they were a relaxed local or a nervous tourist, although in reality few tourists ventured down the narrow alleyways off Calle Montcada. Albert observed a particularly nervous looking tourist who eyed him furtively before rushing away. This incident made Albert consider how unfortunate it was that some tourists were so nervous in this generally safe city. He couldn't understand why someone would take time to visit a place if they were too scared to enjoy the experience. Too many people didn't take the time to enjoy the many architectural and historical delights of this unique area. 'Where does that fear come from?' mused Albert to himself.

'Look!' alerted Christy.

The door to the building they were watching was easing open. Someone was about to leave it. The door opened inwards. The three of them looked towards the action, trying desperately to look inconspicuous at the same time. They didn't want to be seen so they all crammed together into the doorway.

'It's Jorge!' gasped Christy.

She was right. Her sister Vittoria's husband Jorge was the first person to step from behind the door onto the street. He looked around him casually and waited for someone else to follow him through the doorway. As they pressed themselves into the small doorway the three of them all turned away and pretended to be going into the doorway

Reason to Believe

they were standing in. When they looked back at the strange, old building there was no-one in sight.

'Where have they gone?' asked Christy.

There was no answer and no need for one. Instead the three of them rushed along to the corner of the alley and peered around it down the dark and suspicious Carrer de Larc de Sant Vicence. They were just in time to see two men, Jorge and another, turn off the alleyway back into the human melee along Calle Montcada and disappear from view.

The two sisters and Albert stood for a moment rooted to the spot. The three of them seemed helpless until Florita broke the silence.

'Well, what is going on?' she asked.

'Goodness knows, but you two had better keep out of sight as your father may well invite me inside at any moment,' said Albert recovering a little thought and composure.

'OK, we will leave you to it Albert, but you will promise to tell us what is going on, will you not Albert?' instructed Florita in a very fierce voice without consulting her sister.

'Yes of course,' replied Albert, 'Come round to our apartment tonight after nine. I will tell you everything that has happened.'

'Albert! Albert!'

It was the urgent, but hushed voice of Senor Moncada.

Steve Kenning

'It's your Papa. I must go. I will see you tonight,' said Albert quietly as he scurried off back down the alleyway and around the corner to the source of the voice. Christy and Florita watched him go.

'Let's get Julio from school. We can discuss this strange activity thoroughly on the way. Yes?' asked Florita.

'Sure, I really am confused by all this. To be honest Albert also seemed really confused. Yet he's normally so calm,' added Christy.

Senor Moncada welcomed Albert into the two-storey building. He ushered him inside quickly and looked up and down the alley to ensure there was no-one watching. He closed the heavy wooden door. Albert and Senor Moncada stood under a dim light in a large hallway dominated by peeling white walls. The paint was blistered on all the recently painted walls. Most of it had already peeled off and the stone floor was littered with white patches of old paint. He couldn't help himself, but Albert was immediately seduced by the old building, fascinated primarily because there was an unusual wooden staircase that rose up from the stone floor. This was a place he had never before explored. His wide eyes followed the grand wooden structure upwards.

'Come Albert,' instructed the old man.

Reason to Believe

They went up the staircase. At the top the two men passed through a heavy wooden framed doorway and entered a large open room. Albert recognised the large windows covered with metal grills. They were the windows he had seen from the alleyway. The room itself now felt like a narrow, long meeting room, although Albert sensed its previous more recent uses to be more concerned with the storage of something like livestock, and there was no trace of tobacco. As a room it was old, cold and poorly decorated. The plaster on the walls was very old and there were many brown patches of discoloration on the white walls. At the far end of the room were several large tables. All were covered with a range of glass bottles, tubes and other glass objects. Some were filled with liquids and others were empty.

'Look at this Albert,' Senor Moncada gestured towards the laboratory equipment.

'Three years' work.'

Albert walked around the tables looking intently at the glass vessels and their contents. He could smell the chemistry at work.

'What is it?' he asked. Albert was not a chemist.

'This is the result of three years of tests to find a virus,' stated Senor Moncada quietly.

'A virus for what?' asked Albert.

Senor Moncada looked at the floor. His face was grey and he began to look unsteady on his feet. Albert realised immediately that his father-in-law was again in trouble. He stepped over to him and helped the old man to a chair at the edge of the room. Senor Moncada sat down carefully. He still looked grey.

'Albert. I am sorry. I will be sorry until the day I die and I am probably set fair for hell because of my involvement in all this,' he stated with moist eyes.

Albert was at a loss to know what was going on. He said nothing and waited. He needed to hear more. Eventually the old man started to speak.

'It was the idea of Alfonso Carboner. He died an old but very idealistic man in the 1990's. He set the six of us, his remaining followers, a task,' he paused, 'The task was to keep the creed alive and to ensure that the Millenarium succeeded. The plan was simple. We all held the view that we were above everyone else, we were blessed people and that very little could affect us as we were almost holy,' he laughed to himself.

Albert still said nothing. He just listened.

'We were blessed and with this strength we felt that nothing could touch us. Alfonso had instilled a belief in us that there were many bad people in the world that would go straight to hell when they died and that they were probably already in some kind of living hell in this world. The plan was to ensure the success of the Millenarium by developing a virus that would decimate the human population. A virus

Reason to Believe

that would discriminate between those with 'good' souls and those who had sinned considerably.'

Albert understood instantly what the old man was saying and he answered back at him horrified, 'Tell me that it was not you that gave the world the HIV virus. You didn't start AIDS did you?'

Senor Moncada was quick to reply, 'Goodness gracious, no. We were not clever enough to do that,' he halted momentarily thinking, 'However, unfortunately, we are near to developing something equally as bad. Trials have taken place over the past couple of years on animals. They have been successful. The beauty of the virus we have created is that in certain animals it mutates into something different. Sometimes it just fizzles out and sometimes it is quite devastating, turning into something we could not have predicted. You will have heard of bird flu, yes?'

He looked into the eyes of Albert that were filling with disbelief and fear. Albert said nothing.

'We believe bird flu is an offshoot of our TX-778 virus. Anyhow, we are only months away from turning TX-778 into TX-780.'

'So? What is it?' stuttered Albert.

'A human flu virus that will wipe out millions of people.'

'What about you and your families?'

'Ahhh, the beauty is that we believe we are protected by God. Oh, and we do have an antidote,' the old man held his head in his hands, 'I have been such a fool. Now I think I may be too late to stop it all,' wept Senor Moncada.

Albert was confused.

'What has this to do with millenarianism and the orb?'

The old man continued to weep. Albert left him to it whilst he sat still and thought. He was trying to make sense of what he had seen and heard over the past hour. Everything was quite surreal. It was as if he had walked into a nightmare. Albert looked at his father-in-law. He was a hopeless sight. This once grand man, a politician, was reduced to a shrivelled weeping hulk.

'I believed. I felt the power. I thought I was in the presence of something quite divine. I doubt I would feel any different even now if it hadn't been for my operation. The visions started straight afterwards. And it was only when the visions started that I saw that everything I thought was right was so very wrong.'

The old man looked up at Albert, his eyes had stopped crying.

'Albert. I really do need your help. If the work on the virus that I have set in motion with the other millenarianists continues, then not only will I go to hell but the world will too. It is wrong. My visions have shown me that it is wrong. My visions have also shown that you can save us all' he looked at Albert, 'You need to believe me.'

Albert said nothing.

Reason to Believe

The old man thought before speaking again.

'The orb is the force. Without it the Millenarium would end. This work would stop as there would be no point in continuing.'

Albert looked up at his father-in-law and asked the question that was really concerning him.

'What about the orb? What is it? How does it work?'

'It is the heart of God. It is our life force. Without it we have no force or belief. That is exactly why it must be destroyed.'

11

Vittoria, Adrianna and Montse had just slumped onto the L-shaped sofa in Vittoria's smart, minimalistic apartment when Montse's mobile rang. She looked at the caller i.d.

'Florita!' she shouted excitedly into the phone, 'What have you found out?'

Florita quickly summarised the events of the afternoon to Montse in about two minutes. Montse was a little taken aback with the news about Albert and Jorge. She stood momentarily with a vacant look on her face thinking. Then she realised who she was, composed herself and replied dominantly.

Reason to Believe

'I will speak to Albert later but what do you think Jorge was doing there?

'I really don't know. Perhaps we should ask Vittoria?' suggested Florita.

'I will, but what are you doing now?' asked the elder sister.

'Well Albert said he would tell us all about what was going on later this evening,' replied Florita.

'Hmmm, you'd better come over to our apartment then. I'll be there in about twenty minutes. Let yourself in if you beat me there,' said Montse, as eager as anyone to find out from her husband about the afternoon activities of the immediate male members of her family. Montse closed her mobile and turned towards her two other sisters who had been listening keenly.

'What was that all about then?' asked Vittoria.

'What is your husband up to with Papa?' quizzed Montse, taking control of the conversation.

'What do you mean?'

'Florita says that he was coming out of a strange building in the Ciutat Vella this afternoon. A building that Papa was also in.'

Vittoria looked shocked. Adrianna sensed her sisters' discomfort and held her hand.

'What is it Vittoria?' asked Adrianna.

'Well. Jorge is supposed to be away on some kind of conference in Valencia this week. I haven't seen him since Friday last week,' she muttered. Then she deliberately and suddenly changed her demeanour, developing a firm, hard and determined look, 'That's it, he is definitely out of my life.'

'Don't be hasty Vittoria, there may be a very good explanation,' added Montse. She hated relationships ending primarily as she was scared of it ever happening to her.

'What might Jorge be doing in the old part of the city?'

'I don't know. I only found out last year that he was quite religious and that he regularly attended some strange kind of chapel in the Ciutat Vella. He never invited me. This information only came out when I told him to go to hell during an argument. He replied that it was impossible,' said a dejected Vittoria.

'I can just imagine your scientific Jorge saying that in a middle of an argument,' smiled Adrianna.

'Yes, he just looked at me coldly and repeated that God was always with him and that he was guided by God. He said he followed a religion called the Darwinian, or something like that. He left the house at that point and I haven't thought about it until now,' continued Vittoria.

'Well I wonder if that's what he was doing there? Maybe he was simply at his church?' wondered Montse.

'Is Papa religious then?' queried Adrianna.

Reason to Believe

'Yes he always has been. I've no idea what denomination he followed, as he always treated it as a very secretive occupation. He never spoke about it and Mama was never involved. Come to think about it over the years he has always spent a lot of time down in the old city,' said a thoughtful Montse.

The three sisters sat in silence for a few moments reflecting. Then Montse remembered something else.

'I'm sure Albert's grandfather found something out about Papa's activities in the Ciutat Vella. It was many years ago. I remember that he loved the old city but he fell out with Papa over something connected with the Ciutat Vella. I thought it was politics but perhaps it was religion.'

Vittoria was now in tears and not listening to anything or anybody. Adrianna was doing her best to console her sister but with little success. Montse was no use with tears. She didn't do crying and anyway she wanted to talk to Albert. What was going on with Albert, her father and brother in law, Jorge? She was keen to get home and to hear her husband's story of the day. With this in mind Montse decided to take action.

'Adrianna, will you be OK with Vittoria? You are so good with her and I am useless with tears.'

'I know Montse. I will look after her. Go and find out about Papa. Be sure to let me know what is going on,' replied Adrianna sympathetically.

Steve Kenning

'OK, see you later.'

Montse was out of the apartment like a hare out of its trap. As she re-entered the busy street she dialled Albert's mobile number. No answer. It was switched off. He never had his phone off. Now she was worried. What exactly was her husband involved in? Her mind was racing, visually playing a range of scenarios in her mind.

Reason to Believe

12

Albert opened his eyes. He had no idea where he was. It felt as if he had been somewhere else for a while. He could see a white area above him that was interspersed by long wooden beams. Then he realised it was a ceiling. His hands felt the floor on which he lay. It was cold and made of stone. He knew he was on a floor. His mind couldn't tell him where he was, as he recognised nothing. Gradually he recovered his thoughts and he started to piece together his surroundings. He tried to stand up. It took him some time. As he stood on his feet he noticed the laboratory equipment that filled the large room. He looked around until his eyes met those of his father-in-law, Senor Moncada.

Steve Kenning

Now he remembered, he must have fainted. The two men stared deeply into each other's eyes.

'Albert, at last, I was beginning to get worried about you,' uttered Senor Moncada.

'What happened?' asked Albert gingerly, with a hint of embarrassment.

'You must have fainted. The shock of everything I had told you was probably too much for anyone to take, including you.'

Everything he had been told or had seen in recent hours came flooding back to him. He stumbled over to where Senor Moncada was sitting.

'I am too tired and too weak to lift you, so I decided to let you rest. It has been ten minutes or more since you passed out,' added the old man.

Albert felt nauseous. He sat still for a few moments trying to regain his usual composure. The old man just looked at him, waiting patiently with an element of understanding. Eventually he spoke again.

'The dreams or visions I have are a prescient Albert.'

Albert looked at him with a look that said he was confused.

The old man read his mind and continued.

'Prescient means that I can see a possible but very real future. It doesn't mean that it will happen but it could happen if something isn't done to change it. As I said before

Reason to Believe

I have seen many things in the future since my operation, some of which I have changed.'

The old man was clearly very tired, but he was determined to continue to tell Albert as much as he could.

'I have two recurring dreams. They must also be visions because I saw one of them again just a few moments ago when you were unconscious. They get clearer all the time. These two dreams seem to represent opposing scenarios.'

Albert was listening but still feeling unwell.

'The one dream is terrifying. It is Barcelona decimated. People dying on the streets as the medical services are unable to cope with a virus so deadly that virtually no-one survives. I see myself standing above my girls. They lie dead and I am alive.'

At that point he started to weep uncontrollably. Albert looked at this strange man, a man he thought he knew. He reached out to hold his father-in-law. Senor Moncada reacted and pushed Albert's arm away.

'No! I do not deserve your sympathy! I am as much part of this evil scheme as anyone. Only I can stop it however. The others still believe it is the right thing to do to keep the Millenarium dream alive. But they haven't seen my visions.'

'Have you told them?' asked Albert.

'Yes, yes. They think I'm an old crank. They also think I am harmless so they tolerate me. They are determined and driven. The new virus is nearly ready. They plan to release it into the city water supply by the end of the month. We have three weeks.'

Senor Moncada looked up at Albert, his face ashen with fear.

'Do you believe me Albert?'

Albert said nothing but just looked at the face of this man sat a few feet in front of him.

'Do you believe what I have told you?' repeated the old man.

'Yes, I do. I think I do. I don't believe you have never lied to me before. All this is crazy and I feel I am in a dream, but my instinct is to believe you,' answered an exhausted Albert.

The old man sighed with relief.

'Listen carefully Albert. I can only say this once. Partly as I lack the energy to say it twice, but also because it is very dangerous and the others are getting nervous. They will do anything to make sure the plan survives.'

'I am also in danger then?' asked Albert, quickly regaining his usual alertness.

'Unfortunately you are, particularly if you do as I ask of you.'

Albert looked concerned, but decided immediately to support his father-in-law.

'Go on, tell me what you want me to do,' urged Albert.

Reason to Believe

Senor Moncada reached out and held Albert's right hand between his two palms. He looked him straight in the eyes.

'Albert,' he started, 'The other vision I keep having is equally important. It is where you are reading out the words of Fra Dolcino of Novara in the outdoors, I think it is possibly at the Sesia valley in Italy, the birthplace of the Dulcinians and of the idea of the Millenarium. One of my brothers, a priest, is trying to stop you, but you are well supported by my daughters Christy and Montse. You will read and find out about the giant obelisk, but you are not there, instead you are at a graveyard. You find the grave of a follower of Fra Dolcino. It is really his hidden grave, the grave of the great Fra Dolcino, but I cannot read the name on the gravestone in my dream. All I know is that it is a simple headstone by the side of the path that leads to the front of the church. This is important because all the writings I have seen say you must find the grave of Fra Dolcino, yet my vision tells me otherwise. Unfortunately I do not know the name of his disciple.'

Senor Moncada was relieved at having given Albert this much information.

'What happens when I read his words?' asked Albert excitedly.

Steve Kenning

'The orb vanishes. I have seen it happen in my vision. The Millenarium stops and the virus is not released. The Dulcinian priests are defeated.'

The two men stared at each other. Senor Moncada was clearly exhausted. Albert still had more questions.

'What do I read out? Where is the grave?'

Senor Moncada looked forlorn.

'This is the problem Albert. I have seen the end. Good and bad. What I have not seen is the way to provide you with the information you need. All I know is that you are pure enough of soul to bring this evil thing to an end. Understandably you will have to research the Dulcinian movement to find what you need. I simply believed in the ideals, I never was one to find out the history behind it all. It is clear from my dreams that you need to find the words of Fra Dolcino. The words that will end this Millenarian madness.'

Albert felt part excitement and part fear. He felt good about the possibility of being able to do something to save people, and perhaps, he thought amazingly, saving the world made him feel good. Yet he had no idea how he might do this. He looked around him wanting to do something urgently.

'Shall we destroy this equipment?' he said with real intent.

Senor Moncada just shook his head.

Reason to Believe

'That would be so simple. Destroy their experiments, and kill the virus. Unfortunately, this is simply a trial lab. They others have the formulas on computer and there are several different bases for their experiments. We cannot destroy the virus. All we can do is destroy the orb and the source of this Millenarium.'

Senor Moncada was exhausted.

'Albert,' he gasped, 'You must destroy the orb.'

Albert looked at his father in law. The old man's eyes were rolling and he was swaying from side to side in his seat. Albert stood up and lifted the old man to his feet.

'Come on Senor, let's get you home.'

13

'Montse, have you no control over your husband? You tell us all what to do and always appear in control but in reality you don't even know what is going on in your own family. You are my role model for a perfect life but how can I continue to believe in you? You don't know where your husband is or what he is doing. Where is Albert?' stated an exasperated Florita.

All the girls in the Moncada family had now been sitting in the living room of Montse and Albert Puigcerda's apartment for an hour, waiting.

'I have tried to call him several times on his mobile but unusually he has not replied. I am now more worried about

Reason to Believe

Albert than I am worried about Papa,' revealed Montse. Her face was pale and she was visibly and unusually worried.

The girls were all sat in the spacious living room on the array of chairs and sofas that filled the comfortable modern room. The atmosphere was flat. No-one took the lead to improve the mood and no-one seemed to know what to do.

Fifteen long minutes passed before the silence that had enveloped the Puigcerda household was broken when the front door flew open.

'Albert! Papa!' hailed a relieved Montse.

Albert walked into the apartment with an exhausted Senor Moncada in his arms. The sisters immediately sprang to their feet and conducted an unspoken but highly efficient operation to rescue their father from the struggling arms of Albert.

'Put him in that bedroom,' instructed Montse, 'He looks like he needs to lie down.'

As she spoke she followed the other sisters who were carrying their papa into the bedroom. Albert was left alone in the living room. He was dishevelled and very tired. He looked around at the chaos left by his sisters in his living room. They had never been the tidiest of people. He shrugged his shoulders and headed for the grappa in the fridge. The top of the half full bottle came off easily and, after selecting his favourite bevelled grappa glass from a cupboard, he moved slowly from the kitchen back into the living room with the glass of grappa in his hand. Montse at the same time returned from the bedroom having overseen the comfort and wellbeing of her father. She caught site of her husband and for the first time noticed his condition.

'Albert! What has happened to you today? You look terrible!' she remonstrated before changing her approach, 'I have tried to phone you several times.'

The two of them embraced.

'I am so sorry Montse, but it has been the most completely weird day of my life. I need to tell you everything and there is much to tell. You will find some of it very hard to believe, so please bear with me.'

Albert had a solemn and sincere look on his face as he spoke to his bewildered wife.

Montse knew her husband well and was aware that he didn't dramatise anything without good reason. His tone of voice unnerved her and she instantly knew he had had a difficult day. She listened to him, calmly holding his hand as the two of them sat on the sofa. Albert was visibly drawn and his normal exuberance had left his body temporarily. He sat next to Montse on the cream, suede sofa with his grappa in his hand before swigging it down his throat in one go. Montse took the glass from his hand and immediately went to the kitchen to refill it. As she was gone the other sisters filtered back into the sitting room, their father safely asleep.

Reason to Believe

Albert said nothing as the girls sat down around him, looking at him expectantly. After a few minutes of silence Montse returned with a new glass of grappa.

'Do you feel like telling us all about what happened today Albert?' asked Montse carefully. She was fully aware of his character and she could see that he was in a zone of discomfort that was rare for him. She had rarely seen Albert out of his comfort zone.

Albert sat stiffly on the cream sofa. Everyone one else in the room, all five women, all sisters said nothing, they simply stared directly at him. Albert sensed the expectation of the sisters and felt the need to tell someone else about his highly unusual day. He thought for a moment more before announcing, 'OK, you must listen carefully to what I have to say. You may not believe everything I say to you but you must. This is exactly what your father told me.'

Albert paused to take in the initial reactions of the sisters. He looked at them, they were unmoved, so he continued, strangely suddenly determined to grab their interest.

'I must say,' he paused, 'That however surreal and unbelievable all this is, I do actually believe it, however strange it may seem, I did actually see this.'

This comment stunned the women. No-one spoke, they imply looked at their brother-in-law open mouthed. Albert was pleased. He could sense that they wanted to know every detail about his day and just exactly what their Papa had told him. He waited a moment before asking his audience.

'Are you ready?'

They all nodded.

Albert composed himself. Then he began.

'Well, at about 11 a.m this morning I received a call from your father. This was unusual, particularly as he requested to see me later that same day. Usually he arranged things well in advance. When he was speaking to me I sensed a kind of panic in his voice, so I immediately agreed to meet him. Also as he wanted to meet in the old city, I couldn't resist the opportunity.'

Reason to Believe

14

'He has told someone, I am sure. I think he has told Albert,' said Jorge with conviction.

'He has not. He knows the outcome of that. He would not betray our Lord,' replied Jorge's accomplice, a large, bearded man of about forty years of age. He, unlike Jorge, was shabbily dressed. He looked introverted and dishevelled matching the common perception of a scientist who had little time or concern for his appearance. Jorge on the other hand was precise in his every move. His footsteps were neat and economical, his beard clipped to perfection each morning, his hair perfectly groomed. He always looked good.

'Tell me why then, Victor, was my father in law and

Albert Puigcerda in the laboratory? We saw them coming out,' snapped Jorge.

'We didn't see them coming out. We saw your father in law closing the door to the street. He probably arranged to meet Albert outside. Why on earth would he tell anyone of the plan? He is as involved as anyone. He helped put the laboratories together,' stated Victor in a very matter of fact manner.

'No. I am not happy,' responded Jorge, 'Tomeu Moncada has been acting strange recently. Remember straight after his operation he complained of visions? He never said of what, but he was obviously disturbed.'

Victor signed in frustration. He wasn't getting his message across to his friend and colleague. He stroked his beard as he spoke.

'Look Jorge, who was it that got us involved in the Dulcinian Creed?'

Victor paused waiting for an expected response. It didn't arrive.

'It was Tomeu!' he stated after several moments, 'He needed two scientists and with our links with Montserrat, we were the perfect recruits. Your father-in-law has changed our lives. He even briefly introduced us to the wonderful Alfonso Carboner.'

Victor looked to the ground, his body engulfed in sadness.

Reason to Believe

'It was a shame the great man died.'

Victor had lost his train of thought for a second, when he regained it, he stated, 'But, remember, also it was Tomeu who found you a wife, one of his daughters,' he paused again before re-iterating his belief, 'Of course he hasn't told anyone,' stated Victor with conviction.

'Paa,' was all Jorge could say in reply. His mood was obviously unhappy and he stormed up the stairs into the makeshift laboratory.

Unable to agree, the two men set about their work. They both hung up their overcoats in the corner of the room and put on blue cotton medical coats and plastic rimmed goggles. They did not speak to each other for over an hour as they engrossed themselves in their individual tasks. Jorge was seemingly concerned primarily with setting the correct temperature to heat a variety of liquids, whilst Victor was continually looking at chemicals under an electronic microscope before weighing them precisely. After quite some time Jorge spoke again.

'I'm going to follow Tomeu for a while. I think something is wrong.'

Victor looked up in exasperation. He lifted his goggles above his eyes and rested them on his head.

'You are wrong my friend. Even if he had said anything, what could your brother in law, Albert Puigcerda, do to stop us? He is a lawyer. We are three weeks away from our target release date. We have some more tests and refinements to make and we still have to finally complete the antidote. He is too late. He is way too late my friend'

'I just feel it,' pressed Jorge.

'Look,' stated Victor in an attempt to find a halfway solution to this discussion, 'We will tell Ramon, Jordi and Xavi about what we have seen and about your concerns. Let's do that and find out what they think.'

Jorge considered this for a few moments, 'OK. Call them.'

Twenty minutes later five of the remaining six members of the Dulcinian Creed were sitting around a table in an upstairs room in an ancient building on Calle de la Cirera in the heart of the Ciutat Vella. The dim, ancient electric lights hung high above their heads giving the large room a ghostly and mysterious atmosphere.

'I hate this room,' said a huge mountain of a man in his late sixties, conspicuously and dramatically overdressed in a priest's black smock that perfectly matched his shock of thick black hair.

'I thought you would be used to cold, drab buildings Father Jordi,' said Victor with an ironic smile on his face.

'I am but this building has bad memories for me,' responded the white faced Jordi.

'Tell us more,' interjected a thin younger man, well dressed in a fine suit and a thin red tie.

Reason to Believe

'Enough Ramon, we do not need to spend too much time together. The less we are seen as a group the better. We all know our roles and we must stick to them. Our Lord God is relying on us,' said a bearded man wearing thin spectacles. He looked like an esteemed politician with his carefully coiffured grey beard and hair. He was confident and had an aura about him that made the others listen and take heed. As he spoke they all quickly crossed their chests with their right hands.

'Tell us Brother Jorge, what are your concerns about Brother Tomeu?' asked the bearded man.

Jorge shuffled in his seat, 'Well Brother Xavi. I sense that Brother Tomeu has lost his nerve. I think he has lost God's will, I don't think he believes anymore. I also think he has told others of our plans.'

'To what purpose?'

'To stop our work. To stop the Millenarium,' continued Jorge.

The other four men listened with a look of horror on their faces. Victor had heard it all before and scoffed at the suggestion.

'I cannot understand why Brother Tomeu would do such a thing. He was with Jordi and I when we first met Alfonso Carboner, was he not, when we were mere teenagers? Alfonso was our guiding light, our master; he led us through our lives. Tomeau was part of the planning team for the Millenarium action. Why would he do such a thing? He is one of God's servants. He has the strongest reason to believe,' said a surprised Xavi.

'I know. I have much to thank Tomeu for, but I am also one of God's servants and I aim to complete his work, nothing can stop it. However, I ask you all to think about it. Brother Tomeu has been acting very strangely since his operation. He is not the man he was,' continued Jorge.

'But he is very old. What do you expect?' questioned Jordi.

The men sat there considering Jordi's words. They were not a group of people who took rash and rapid decisions. They were careful and methodical. Eventually Xavi spoke, 'I find all this very hard to believe Brother Jorge. Yet our project on behalf of our Lord is very special and nothing can get in the way of its success. We must not ignore your concerns.'

He thought about his next words.

'This is what we will do. Jorge you investigate your father in laws recent movements. I will talk to him. Ok?' he looked at the others. They all nodded.

'OK, let's go. We have no time to lose.'

Reason to Believe

15

Albert was still drinking grappa although the sisters had opened a bottle of red wine and were deep in discussion following their brother-in-laws tales of the day's events. There had been a slight sense of disbelief at first but as Albert progressed into the story, the sisters all started to piece together quirky aspects of their father's life and behaviour over the years that slowly confirmed the validity of the day's events in their minds. Albert was surprised but pleased. They trusted him impeccably and believed his every word.

'The main thing is to make sure that Papa is alright,' said Adrianna.

Steve Kenning

'Oh, he will be fine. I will take him for a check up at the hospital tomorrow morning. What we need to do is stop Jorge and his colleagues. Whoever they are,' said a fiercely determined Florita.

Vittoria looked embarrassed at the mention of her husband.

'Oh, I'm so sorry. I had no idea that Jorge could be involved in this kind of thing,' she uttered defensively.

'But you did have some idea that he was up to something Vittoria, but what could you do?' added Adrianna supportively.

'I didn't think he was into this kind of thing. I had no idea,' responded Vitoria.

Christy ignored her frivolous sister.

'I think we need to find out about this Dulcinian Creed. We need to find out what Albert needs to say to stop this madness and where he has to say it,' she announced, attempting to point them in the right direction, 'Just in case it is all true.'

'But what if Papa is just making it all up? Maybe he is becoming senile?' questioned Florita, she had obviously suddenly had a change of heart as well as quickly making her mind up about the whole situation.

'I cannot spend time on this. I have an election to fight. I think Papa is in the early stages of senile dementia. We

Reason to Believe

should get him checked out before we take his stories any further.'

Christy was visibly surprised by Florita's outburst.

'How can you say that? Albert saw the orb and if Papa is telling the truth nothing will matter, not even your election,' replied Christy.

'I can't take that risk. I think everything Albert has told us is true, although I cannot account for the floating orb thing he saw or why the laboratory is there, but I really can't believe that anyone is sick enough to poison the world,' continued Florita in a very matter of fact tone of voice.

'Didn't something like this happen in Japan? Some terrorist group pumped poison gas into the metro,' added Vittoria.

'Yes and where do all these strange flu viruses come from come from? They could be manufactured by terrorists,' added Adrianna.

Montse hadn't said much up to now. She had sat and listened carefully considering the best course of action. She knew she had to enter the debate.

'I hear all you are saying but we have no real proof either way of what is going on. I really believe in Albert and if he is convinced about what he saw and by what he was told, then so am I. I really don't agree with you Florita. I think you want to stick your head in the sand and I am surprised at you. We need to do something otherwise we may live to regret it. I know we have to do something. It is the orb that I cannot understand. It sounds so incredible. It can only be true,' she said. The others listened. Albert looked at his wife with interest. She always had interesting things to say and she was nearly always right.

There was a lull in the conversation. Florita looked hurt by her sisters' reactions and the others were numbed by Christy's harsh words.

Then Montse erupted, virtually jumping from her chair to announce the course of action she felt they should all follow.

'Albert and I will take a few days off from work to find out what we need to know about this organisation and whatever millenarianism is. Can anyone else spare anytime?'

'I can, if someone can look after my boy,' added Christy.

'That would be a pleasure,' added Vittoria, 'I love your boy, but I would be useless investigating this cult,' she stated, then she thought a little and added, 'Particularly as one of it's most weird members is my husband.

The room was quiet for a few seconds as they allowed Vittoria's short rant to subside, then Adrianna spoke to bring things back to the focus of the conversation.

'I'm with you Vittoria. I would be much better looking after Julio than searching for information. Vittoria and I will look after your boy.'

Reason to Believe

'Florita,' quizzed Montse, 'Are you out of this?'

Florita nodded silently trying to disappear.

Again there was a pause before anyone else spoke as if no one was keen to move things further. Then Montse took the lead, as was usual.

'OK, lets go with this. Christy, bring Julio over here and the girls can stay here to look after him. Are you two OK with that?'

Adrianna and Vittoria snuggled up to each other and smiled at the thought of the combined challenge of looking after their sister's boy. Adrianna knew that it would help take Vittoria's mind off her problems with her husband, Jorge.

'Great. Come on Vittoria, let's go get our things,' said Adrianna getting up and looking towards Vittoria.

Both Vittoria and Christy got up simultaneously to go in their own directions.

'Good. Let's meet back here in an hour,' confirmed Montse, satisfied with her sisters acceptance of her directives designed to establish some kind of order.

16

The thin red second hand on a white electric clock stuttered clockwise between the thicker black hands. It was 9 p.m. The clock hung on the brick wall of the cavernous central hall of the main library at the Universitat de Pompei Fabrega. It was less than an hour from closing time but time was of no concern to them. Christy seemed to be on good terms with most people in the city and a professor friend had given the three of them permission to start their research in the library that looked onto the picturesque Calle de Wellington.

The time was irrelevant but they were still in a hurry, so Christy, Montse and Albert quickly divided up the research tasks. Christy would use the internet to access some of the

Reason to Believe

specialist research sites that only universities seemed to have access to. Albert's job was to search the texts, while Montse was to look through the libraries own stored records that were kept on disk. On the way over to the library in Christy's car the three of them had tried to work out a focus for their research to both save time and to discover the maximum information. It wasn't hard to decide on their main area of research as they had very little knowledge of the subject area. All they knew about the Dulcinian sect was what Senor Moncada had told Albert. They decided that there were three areas to research. These were the Dulcinian sect, including Fra Dolcino, millenarianism and Alfonso Carboner. It was unanimously agreed that they would all look for the Dulcinian creed as a starting point.

It didn't take long to get a lead. Christy, using the internet, immediately found a site with a good amount of information relating to the Dulcinian movement. She called Montse over to her and soon the two sisters were looking at the LCD screen in an alcove overlooking the tram tracks of Calle de Wellington. They left Albert to the libraries millions of books, as they assumed he was probably quite some distance away from them.

'Look here Montse,' said Christy pointing to the screen

'Dottrina religiosa Utilitaria Di Dulcinian,' were the words printed in black on a document revealed on the computer.

115

Steve Kenning

'That must mean the doctrine of the Utilitarian Dulcinian movement,' stated Montse, 'translate the page. It must be in Italian.'

Christy pressed a few keys on the keyboard and the page flicked up in an understandable language. The two women were eager to read. They leaned forward towards the screen.

'Utilitarian Dulcinian Creed. The Dulcinian religious movement was inspired by Franciscan ideals, influenced by the Joachimites and derived from the Apostolics. It was led by Fra Dolcino of Novara (1250-1307), who was burnt as a heretic in 1307 on the orders of Pope Clement.

The Dulcinian movement began in 1300 when Gherardo Segarelli, founder of the Apostolics sect, was burned in Parma. A brutal repression of the movement followed and his followers had to hide to save their lives. Fra Dolcino, who had joined the movement between 1288 and 1292, took over the role of a leader of the sect.

At first they settled in the lower parts of the Seisa Valley in Northern Italy and were enthusiastically welcomed by the inhabitants. Here the movement grew (the number reported again vary from a few hundreds to 4000 members and even 15000) as escaped serfs and scholars from various parts of Italy joined them. Soon the troops of the Bishops of Novara and Vercelli attacked them and they were forced to move to higher ground, helped by some of the inhabitants of the valley. They were repeatedly

Reason to Believe

attacked and fled again, suffering great losses. At the end of 1304 only 1400 (4000 according to other sources) Apostolics survived on the fortified Piano dei Gazzari (m 1426) on the top of Mount Parete Calva. They descended from the mountain only to depredate and kill the inhabitants of the valley responsible in their eyes for not having defended them enough against the troops of the Bishops. At this point the people started to call them "Gazzari" (from Cathars) and joined the troops in an attempt to defeat them.

Dolcino justified everything committed by the Dulcinians in this period by affirming that they were so perfect they could do anything they wanted without Sin, basing his affirmation on Saint Paul (Epistle to Titus 1,15): 'To the pure all things are pure, but to the corrupt and unbelieving nothing is pure; their very minds and consciences are corrupted.'

In the mean time Pope Clement V in 1306 called for a crusade to finally crush the movement and troops from various parts of northern Italy joined the siege of the mountain. The Dulcinians could no longer descend the mountain to find food but they resisted for a year eating rats, horses, dogs and in some cases practicing cannibalism, after a final assault in 1307 when many (some sources say 800) Dulcinians were killed they finally surrendered and 150 of them were captured and later executed. *Margherita of Trento and Dolcino were captured alive and brought to the nearby Biella where Margherita was burned at the stake on the 1st of June 1307.*

Little was heard of the movement until in 1907, on the 600th anniversary of the martyrdom, huge celebrations were held in the Sesia Valley and a 12 metre high obelisk was posted in the place of their last resistance. This obelisk was destroyed by Fascists in 1927, and a small monument was built on this site in 1974 by a small group of religious fanatics who had converted to the Dulcinian beliefs. These fanatics had no connection with the Seisa Valley, or indeed with Italy, they were young, well-educated religious zealots who had been looking for a movement that had religious ideals but also incorporated a relevance to the changing European politics of the mid-twentieth century. These new Dulcinians were disgruntled and disillusioned with the growing corruptness and the waning influence of the Christian Church. They wanted to save the world from evil. This strange mixture of young men, a collection from France, Spain and Germany, set about constructing their movement in the foothills of the Spanish Pyrenees. There at a place called Pardines, they constructed an obelisk above, according to modern legend in the Sesia Valley, the bones of Fra Dolcino. Old men in the valley talk of disturbances around the grave of Fra Dolcino in the early 1970's and of how suddenly on the construction of this new symbol of the

Reason to Believe

Dulcinian movement the poverty of the valley, that had lasted for the past few hundred years, had lifted virtually overnight.'

As the two sisters finished reading the text almost simultaneously they looked at each other with a sense of excitement.

'Print it out. Print it out,' squealed Montse in excitement, 'Albert needs to see this.'

'It gives us a good start, doesn't it?' added Christy, 'We need to corroborate this evidence by finding other sources but at least we know who the Dulcinians were.'

'OK. You print it Christy and I will find Albert. This is probably all we can do here tonight. We may as well head home, we can continue on the internet there.'

Montse left Christy to the computer and headed off excitedly between the rows of books and periodicals in search of her husband.

17

The darkness of the night outside appeared to be slowly engulfing the old, cavernous room in which the five men were seated around a rectangular dark wooden table. The room was partially illuminated by a few small electric candle type lights that clung to the stonewalls of at intermittent intervals, although the dim light they emanated was losing an unwinnable battle against the encroaching darkness. There was no moon in the sky that night. The mood of the five men reflected the darkness of the night. None of them were speaking. Each one was hunched forward leaning their head in their hands. They had been in this state for over an hour.

Reason to Believe

After several more minutes of this inner reflection, wrestling with the predicament they now found themselves in, the bearded, bespectacled Xavi spoke. He was the natural leader of this leaderless group.

'OK then. We know that Brother Tomeu brought your brother-in-law,' as he spoke he signalled his attentions towards Jorge, 'Albert to this building. Yes?'

Jorge quickly responded, 'Yes. According to Senora Almiral they entered the building this afternoon and left about half an hour later. She sees everything that woman.'

'And, Victor, you tell me that they also went upstairs in the Palace earlier?'

'Our friend Senor Batista at the café in the Textile Museum saw them go up the staircase and enter the building,' responded Victor.

'Eeurgh!' exhaled an exasperated Xavi, 'Why? What is Tomeu playing at? I have known him for over fifty years. He is my best friend. Why tell someone about our work? Especially at this time,' continued Brother Xavi, his carefully coiffured appearance unruffled by his mood.

Ramon, still sharply dressed in his business suit offered a thought.

'Perhaps he is trying to get Albert to join us?'

'No, we would all have to agree to that, but anyway Albert is not the type,' added Victor.

'That is true,' agreed Jorge, 'He has no religious base.'

Steve Kenning

More silence.

'What do you mean?' asked Ramon after some thought.

'He is very moralistic but he does not believe in God. Never has. Never will.'

Father Xavi looked questioningly at Jorge, he was keen to move the conversation on.

'Victor tells me that your wife has left you Jorge, is that true?'

'Huh? Oh, yes she has, although I only found out this morning. She left me a note saying she was staying with one of her sisters for a while,' Jorge replied nervously.

'So what you are saying is that we now don't have any inside information as to what your family are doing?' questioned Brother Xavi.

Jorge looked embarrassed and said nothing.

'Can you not get her back?' asked Victor.

'No. This is not the first time she has left, and to be honest, I don't want her back. It won't matter soon anyway. The future is for those that believe. She has never shared my beliefs.'

The other four men nodded knowingly in agreement in the gloom.

The huge black haired man in the priests robe had been sitting quietly listening and thinking. Then he spoke, 'It all appears fairly clear to me.'

The others looked at him.

Reason to Believe

'What does Father Jordi?' asked Victor.

'It appears that Brother Tomeu has, for some reason, lost his nerve,' he paused, 'This Albert is a good man is he not?'

'Yes, he is very good. I would trust him implicitly, as would anyone who had met him,' answered Jorge.

'Then it is clear that brother Tomeu believes Albert is the man destined to stop the Millenarium.'

A look of horror shuddered across the faces of the men sitting at the table at the mere thought of their mission being stopped. They sat and thought. One by one their expressions clearly revealed the realisation that Father Jordi was possibly right in his assumptions.

'Go on,' instructed Brother Xavi, 'Tell us exactly what you are thinking Father Jordi.'

Before the priest could speak, Victor, clearly agitated, blurted out a statement, 'Why? Why would Brother Tomeu put everything at risk?'

'Let us just think for a moment about Brother Tomeu,' responded Father Jordi calmly.

Father Jordi was in his late sixties, although he looked incredibly strong, powerful and fit. His face was weathered brown. Even the deep grooves of his countless wrinkles were seared brown. These features were the most evident result of years spent undertaking pilgrimages walking across the scorched lands of the Iberian Peninsula in search of salvation. The creases around his eyes and mouth represented hardship and he probably looked far older than he actually was. This was a deeply religious man. He had known no other life other than the life he had led under the influence of his God.

'We are all men of God. We are all true Christians and we believe wholeheartedly in our work to rid this world of evil. We can see the work of the Devil in every aspect of our society. Walk through the streets of Barcelona and there is the decadence of evil everywhere. However, not everyone is as enlightened or should I say, as mentally strong as we are. We are our Lords disciples and our mission is to maintain the faith.'

As Father Jordi spoke he emanated an aura of holiness. He truly believed in what he was saying. The other four men were entranced and listened to his words still and in awe.

'Despite our beliefs we have to accept that there are other 'good' people in this world. These people also have power from sources we do not understand. I wonder if this Albert is indeed deeply religious without realising it. Remember that our Lord Jesus was in fact a Jew and the religious elders of that time could not understand his actions. Perhaps Albert is a messenger of our Lord. Our Lord does after all work in mysterious ways.'

'So what are you saying Father Jordi?' asked Brother Xavi, 'That we should let this Albert do what he has to do?'

Reason to Believe

Father Jordi turned towards Xavi and spoke sternly, 'Not at all. This is a test. The Lord has sent us a messenger to test our resolve. We need to take this challenge and ensure the Millenarium survives. This is our destiny.'

With these words Father Jordi spread out his arms towards the men on either side of him. He took hold of their hands. Within seconds the small group of men were sitting in a circle, holding hands. Father Jordi was building their belief. They all felt righteous, strong and purposeful.

'Believe in our Lord Brothers. We are on this Earth to do his work. We have nearly completed our task. We must succeed or the Earth is doomed. Our Lord made this wonderful place teeming with a diversity of life and put man on the Earth to look after his creation. Man has let the Lord down. The time is right to cull humankind and to give the Earth back to nature. Those of us who survive will have a very different approach to the management of this planet. We have the reason to believe! We are the chosen ones!'

The mantra moved the group. Jorge was in tears and Xavi started shouting, 'Save us Lord, save us!'

The room was flooded with emotion and energy. Each man was fully engaged with the belief that he was immortal. There was a frenzy of words, emotions and hysterical activity. Eventually Brother Xavi recovered some semblance of control.

Steve Kenning

'Enough for now Brothers! We need to think clearly and carefully about how we move forward. We will meet here at nine tomorrow morning.'

With these words the small party gradually dissolved into their own individual worlds.

Reason to Believe

18

The library at the University on Calle Wellington was a grand building. In the daylight its high, brick walls and tall windows revealed its recent past as some sort of industrial artefact sitting on the edge of the old industrial district of Poble Nou. As the three of them, Albert, Montse and Christy stood outside the grand building waiting for it to open, the eight a.m tram rolled by efficiently behind them.

'I love this road. Look at the trees,' stated Christy.

The other two briefly took in the vista. On one side of the half-mile long road ran a wall that hid the Ciutadella Park and zoo. The other side at the mid-point was the University building. The road was fifty metres wide with a double, grass filled, tram track running down the middle. The beauty of this road was entirely due to the avenue of elm trees that framed the entirety of Calle Wellington. Albert liked it although there were not enough ancient buildings for it to entrance him.

'It is nice,' was all he could muster, although he was very sympathetic to Christy's view.

Montse wasn't interested. Pretty, nice and sweet were words not found in her vocabulary. She liked reality. She loved to have a concrete task. Now, with their real need to act quickly and decisively in relation to the threat posed by the Dulcinian creed, she was fully armed and ready for action. Nothing else was on her mind, as a result, she was completely focussed.

'It really is important for us to solve this problem. Albert and Christy, do you understand how important our task is?'

Albert and Christy were engaged in enjoying the sunshine and the tranquil environment of Calle Wellington. They were oblivious to the intensity of Montse.

'Well?' repeated an irritated Montse, when neither of them responded.

Suddenly sensing a change in the climate, Albert was first to respond, fully aware of exactly what the tone of voice used by his wife actually meant.

'Well yes, but we don't exactly know just how important it is. At the moment we only have the words of your father to go on.'

Reason to Believe

This was the wrong thing to say. Montse erupted and hurled words of admonishment at her husband.

'Do you doubt Papa? He has never lied. You saw the state he was in. He is in turmoil. I spoke to him again last night and he implored us to resolve this situation immediately. He said we have no more than a couple of weeks. Papa never lies.'

Albert quickly realised his mistake and backtracked.

'Montse I agree. I want to resolve this as well. If nothing else it will act as a form of absolution for your father.'

Montse was about to argue further with her husband when Christy took the opportunity to move things forward.

'Look you two, the library is open. Let's get a coffee and decide on what exactly we need to find.'

Within five minutes each of them had a coffee in their hand and they were sitting around a large, rectangular table on the ground floor of the library. There was no one else around.

'Ok,' said Christy, 'Last night gave us a good start. Today though we need to find several things. I think we need to find out more about millenarianism, exactly where the village of Pardines is in the Pyrenees and we also need to know how to turn off the orb.'

'That is the hard one,' stated Albert, 'Exactly how will we find the words to be spoken to destroy the orb? Your father told me of his vision. He said that in his vision I was reading out the words of Fra Dolcino of Novara at the Sesia valley in Italy, the birthplace of both the Dulcinians and of the idea of the Millenarium. He also said hat in his vision we were just ahead of a priest who was trying to kill me, but when this happened we were not in front of the giant obelisk but at the graveyard of a follower of Fra Dolcino. Your papa went on to say that he believed this grave to actually be that of Fra Dolcino, his hidden grave. He said it was a simple headstone by the side of the path that led to the front of the church.'

'Hmmm,' uttered Christy, 'Not knowing the place or anything about this movement makes this whole task really difficult.'

The coffee wasn't helping to lift their spirits. This was an enormous task. Montse sensed the despair in the air but she was not having any of it.

'So we need to find the words of Fra Dolcino and some information about the village of Pardines,' directed Montse, 'Albert your good on places. You look for this village. Christy you are superb at finding things on the internet and we really need to find the words of Fra Dolcino. Can you look for them? I will find out about the Millenarium movement. Have we all got our mobiles on? This is a big place lets get to work!'

Montse had galvanised them into action. They each had their instructions, and now there was a real sense of urgency amongst the three. There was no questioning the logic of Montse. They were keen to find the information they needed quickly and this gave them all a real momentum. They separated and set to work.

Montse was perfectly right in her judgement of her sister Christy. She was indeed excellent at finding things on the internet. Within several minutes of her work on the web, after being attached to a computer on the top floor of the library, she had found what she was looking for. She had found the words of Fra Dolcino, or at least the next best thing to them. Christy picked up her mobile and called Montse.

'Montse! Montse! I have found his words.'

'Who? Fra Dolcino?'

'Yes. Come and see. I'm on the first floor.'

'Tell Albert. I'm on my way.'

Christy called Albert and within a couple of minutes all three of them were looking at the LCD screen that was placed just in front of Christy. She had found several pages that were of particular interest. The first stated very clearly from some eighteenth century research that had apparently never been proven incorrect, that none of the words of Fra Dolcino had ever been recorded. He was a warrior and not an orator. He said little and expected his deeds to count for his words. The second screen she had on her computer revealed a record of the actions of Fra Dolcino and his followers. As the three of them studied the text there was little to enthuse them, it was merely a report of the battles they fought and the eventual capture and execution of Fra Dolcino. Albert stepped away from the screen in frustration.

'Oh Christy. You had me excited. I thought you had found something important. You said you had found the words of Fra Dolcino. These are the words we need to find. This is rubbish!' argued Albert in exasperation.

Christy was unmoved. She spoke clearly and with a smile on her face.

'I have found the words Albert. Look!'

She clicked onto another screen. There were the words they were looking for. The section, from an old translated text they were looking at, was prefaced by an explanation by the Utilitarian Dulcinian Creed. The article stated: *'The soul of Fra Dolcino lies here amongst the bones of his followers Carpisam and Galinioso. Our small congregation has taken his soul and given it life amongst these beautiful mountains where it will be undisturbed. The soul of Fra Dolcino will live on and give life to the next Millenarium. We witness on this day a great holiness who reignite the life and the work of Fra Dolcino with these words:*

'Thou who perchance,
Shalt shortly view the sun, this warning thou,
Bear to Dolcino – bid him, if he wish not
Here soon to follow me, that with good store,

Reason to Believe

Of food he arm him, lest imprisoning snows
Yield him a victim to Novara's power
No easy conquest else.'

We are not alone in our quest. There are eight of us sworn to establish the new Millenarium although our belief is strengthened by the words of the great poet Dante:

"More than a hundred were there when they heard him,
Who in the moat stood still to look at me,
Through the wonderment oblivious of their torture.
Now say to Fra Dolcino, then, to arm him,
Thou, who perhaps wilt shortly see the sun,
if soon he wish not here to follow me,
so with provisions, that no stress of snow
may give the victory to the Novarese,
which otherwise to gain would not be easy".
The Divine Comedy – Inferno:Canto XXVIII

We are truly indebted to the inspiration of this great man. There can be no question that we are on the right course.

At the bottom of the last page was an indication of their origin, 'The diary of Alfonso Carboner.'

Montse, Christy and Albert looked at each other in amazement. It had been so easy to find the words. Christy said what the other two were thinking.

Steve Kenning

'Someone within the Dulcinian creed must have been so proud of what they were doing that they simply put the diary of Alfonso Carboner onto the internet.'

'The words must be exactly as originally stated,' said Montse.

'Well done Christy,' was all Albert could muster.

'Ok, let's find the other information we need,' urged Montse, 'Christy, you help me.'

The next two hours passed slowly as the three of them searched for the information they needed. Some leads were followed but resulted in nothing. Eventually Christy again found something of interest. Searching the bookshelves she had found a huge historical volume of religious European history. She carried it along several aisles before she found Montse.

'Look Montse! This seems to be a definitive history of millenarianism. What do you think?'

She put the text in front of her sister.

The main concepts of the Dulcinian Heresy were:

* The fall of the ecclesiastical hierarchy and return of the Church to its original ideals of humility and poverty.

* The fall of the Feudal system which oppressed the people.

* Human liberation from any restraint and from entrenched power.

Reason to Believe

* Creation of a new egalitarian society based on mutual aid and respect, holding property in common and respecting equality between sexes.

Millenarian groups typically claim that the current society and its rulers are corrupt, unjust, or otherwise wrong. They therefore believe they will be destroyed soon by a powerful force. The harmful nature of the status quo is always considered intractable without the anticipated dramatic change.

In the modern world economic rules or vast conspiracies are seen as generating oppression. Only dramatic change will change the world and change will be brought about, or survived, by a group of the devout and dedicated. In most millenarian scenarios, the disaster or battle to come will be followed by a new, purified world in which the true believers will be rewarded.

While many millennial groups are pacifist, millenarian beliefs have been claimed as causes for people to ignore conventional rules of behaviour, which can result in violence directed inwards (such as mass suicides) and/or outwards (such as terrorist acts). It sometimes includes a belief in supernatural powers or predetermined victory.

Although never officially recognised by the Catholic Church, millennialism, which had clearly already existed in Jewish thought, received a new interpretation and fresh impetus with the arrival of Christianity. A millennium is a period of one thousand years, and, in particular, Christ's thousand-year rule on this earth, either directly preceding or immediately following the Second Coming (and the Day of Judgement).

The millennium reverses the previous period of evil and suffering; it rewards the virtuous for their courage while punishing the evil-doers, with a clear separation of saints and sinners. The vision of a thousand-year period of bliss for the faithful, to be enjoyed here on earth ("heaven on earth"), exerted an irresistible power Throughout the ages, hundreds of sects were convinced that the millennium was imminent, about to begin in the very near future, with precise dates given on many occasions.

Making use of the dogma of the Trinity, the Italian monk and theologian Joachim of Fiore (d. 1202) claimed that all of human history was a succession of three ages:

1. The Age of the Father (the Old Testament)

2. The Age of the Son (the New Testament)

3. The Age of the Holy Spirit (the age of love, peace, and freedom)

It was believed that the Age of the Holy Spirit would begin at around 1260, and that from then on all believers would be living as monks, mystically transfigured and full of praise for God, for a thousand years until Judgement Day would put an end to the history of our planet.

Reason to Believe

In the Modern Era, with the impact of religion on everyday life gradually decreasing and eventually almost vanishing, some of the concepts of millennial thinking have found their way into various secular ideas, usually in the form of a belief that a certain historical event will fundamentally change human society

The most controversial interpretation of the Three Ages philosophy and of millennialism in general is Hitler's "Third Reich" ("Drittes Reich", "Tausendjähriges Reich"), which, in his vision, would last for a thousand years - but which in reality only lasted for 12 years (1933-1945).

The phrase "Third Reich" was coined by the German thinker Arthur Moeller van den Bruck, who in 1923 published a book entitled Das Dritte Reich, which eventually became a catchphrase that survived the Nazi regime.

Looking back at German history, two periods were distinguished:

*   * The Holy Roman Empire (beginning with Charlemagne in AD 800) (the "First Reich"), and*

*   * The German Empire under the Hohenzollern dynasty (1871 - 1918) (the "Second Reich").*

These were now to be followed, after the interval of the Weimar Republic (1918 - 1933), during which constitutionalism, parliamentarism and even pacifism ruled, by:

*The "Third Reich" of Adolf Hitler.

In a speech held on 27 November 1937, Hitler commented on his plans to have major parts of Berlin torn down and rebuilt:

"Einem tausendjährigen Volk mit tausendjähriger geschichtlicher und kultureller Vergangenheit für die vor ihm liegende unabsehbare Zukunft eine ebenbürtige tausendjährige Stadt zu bauen."

"To build a millennial city adequate [in splendour] to a thousand year old people with a thousand year old historical and cultural past, for its never-ending [glorious] future."

Still waiting.

The name is from the 20th chapter of the Book of Revelations. Christ has just defeated the Beast, and cast him and his false prophet into a "lake of fire burning with brimstone". Christ has also slaughtered the army of the beast, including the kings of the earth, slaying them with a sword, which "proceeded out of his mouth".

And I saw an angel come down from heaven, having the key of the bottomless pit and a great chain in his hand. And he laid hold on the dragon, that old serpent, which is the Devil, and Satan, and bound him a thousand years, and cast him into the bottomless pit, and shut him up, and set a

Reason to Believe

seal upon him, that he should deceive the nations no more, till the thousand years should be fulfilled: and that that he must be loosed a little season. And I saw thrones, and they sat upon them, and judgement was given unto them: and I saw the souls of them that were beheaded for the witness of Jesus, and for the word of God, and which had not worshipped the beast, neither his image, neither had they received his mark upon their foreheads, or in their hands; and they lived and reigned with Christ a thousand years. But the rest of the dead lived not again until the thousand years were finished. This is the first resurrection. Blessed and holy is he that hath part in the first resurrection: on such the second death hath no power, but they shall be priests of God and of Christ, and shall reign with him a thousand years (Historically, it seems that the Beast was the Emperor Nero, whose reign the author of Revelations was enduring.).

The appeal of such a belief to those who feel themselves the victims of injustice and oppression is manifest, and, as a matter of historical fact, most people have been victims of injustice and oppression. Even beyond that, it can speak, very powerfully, to longings for a decisively better order of things, one without the all-too-evident imperfections of the present, one, moreover, untainted by connection with the present order.

Steve Kenning

Montse looked at her sister. It was obvious that they were thinking the same thing.

'It is true. Papa is right. They are going to destroy the world. This Dulcinian Utilitarian Creed he belongs to believe they are blessed and that all evil should be destroyed,' Montse spouted.

'They think they are going to save the world,' added Christy.

'We have got to stop them. Come on Christy. Let's find Albert.

Reason to Believe

19

'I followed them this morning,' said the short black bearded man with apprehension in his voice as if he was waiting for approval. He looked around at his small audience before continuing, 'Montse, Albert's wife, Albert and his wife's sister sister, Christy. The three of them, I was outside their, Montse and Albert's, apartment as that is where Vittoria is staying,' reported Jorge with no sense of emotion.

'Do you miss Vittoria? It sounds as if you are sad,' commented Father Jordi provocatively.

Jorge looked down at the table as he spoke, 'No, I think you can tell by my manner that I do not miss her, however,

Steve Kenning

I do have concerns for her. I have been married to her for a few years after all.'

He looked up at the others maintaining a strong stare.

'Anyway, I followed the three of them to the Pompeu Fabreu University library on Calle de Wellington. They were in there for a long time. I would think they were searching for information on our work, although I have no evidence of that.'

'Why do you not know exactly what they were doing there?' asked Brother Xavi with a sense of exasperation in his voice.

Jorge looked sheepish, quietly replying, 'I could not get into the library.'

From his demeanour it was obvious there was something he was holding back. Brother Xavi drilled him silently with his eyes and waited for a response. Jorge relented, 'OK, I was banned last year for a disturbance I caused there, so I couldn't get in.'

The others decided not to press him for further information on this issue, as there was obviously nothing to be gained. Instead they turned to more immediate concerns.

'We need to take action. If they are looking into our organisation we will need to do something about it,' said Brother Xavi.

'We do not know if they are looking into our work, although I guess it is very likely. To be perfectly honest I

Reason to Believe

believe our biggest problem is Brother Tomeu. He knows everything about our work. After all he was central to the development of our creed, was he not? I can only wonder at what must he have told them already?' commented a worried Victor.

Brother Xavi clasped his hands together deliberately in front of his chest calmly before quietly replying, 'Brother Tomeu will be of no further concern to us. God's will has made sure of that,' he looked towards Father Jordi before continuing, 'I am right am I not Father Jordi, Brother Tomeu has passed on to our Lord.'

Father Jordi's face was hard and expressionless. He nodded.

No one said a word. It was if the whole world had shuddered for a millisecond. All of a sudden it dawned on them that this activity they were engaged in was for real. A brother was dead. The three others in the creed all knew what Brother Xavi meant. They were suddenly scared at the enormity of what they had become embroiled in and hung their heads in quiet respect for a lost brother.

Several minutes passed in the dark and musty room. The brothers had tried over the years to brighten up and lighten the mood of the first floor loft but to no avail. Regardless of their efforts the place still stank of stale straw, despite the fact that there had probably been no straw in the place for over a hundred years, and it was always dark.

Steve Kenning

Eventually Victor spoke, 'We have to succeed,' he hesitated, then looked for reassurance in the faces of his Brothers, 'Don't we? There is no going back.'

He sounded a little helpless, looking for guidance. All five of them knew he was right. Whatever else happened they were all implicated by the death of Brother Tomeu, there was no going back. Brother Xavi's actions had ensured their loyalty until the end.

Father Jordi sensed the others needed the spiritual uplift he believed it was his role in life to provide.

'Life is what you make of it,' he suggested, 'And our lives will be fulfilled by fulfilling God's will. Just think of our reception in heaven.'

For once, the others, with the exception of Brother Xavi, had a bemused, slightly unbelieving look on their faces. Father Jordi and Brother Xavi were the hardcore survivors from the early days with Alfonso Carboner. They were completely enraptured by his wisdom and vision. There was no alternative to the course of action they had taken. The others, Jorge, Victor and Ramon had been more recent recruits to the movement. Not one of them had been fully entrapped by the charisma of Alfonso Carboner, they had hardly known him and most of their belief had been instilled in them by their older Brothers. They had all been drawn in by the philosophy and ideals proported by Brother Xavi. However, with the bitterness of the reality of Brother

Reason to Believe

Tomeu's untimely death, the three others looked at each other with a lack of surety.

A pall of uneasy silence gripped the room. No one was speaking or wanted to speak although the sense of concern was palatable, this uneasy atmosphere was carefully changed by Brother Xavi. He knew he had to say something to brighten the mood in order to lessen the obvious concern of the others.

'You are all worried my friends. I sense your thoughts. Things are now getting very serious. As soon as Brother Tomeu's activities were confirmed, if we are honest with ourselves, we knew things would change. Now it is a time for true believers to act. If any of you feel that you are not strong enough to follow God's will I personally will understand. I am prepared to take responsibility for Brother Tomeu's death, with God's support, and to not implicate any of you. At the same time I am prepared to let you walk away from our plan if the pressure is too much for any of you.'

He was half standing and paused deliberately to study each of his Brothers in turn. When he was ready he continued, 'However, if you do walk away you must resolve to say nothing and to suffer with the other sinners when our Lord's plan comes to fruition. The choice is yours.'

This last sentence was said with some venom and carried an obvious threat. No one said a word. No expressions betrayed their moods. They just sat there. There was nothing else to say. Father Jordi was completely devoid of any rational thought outside of his religion and was totally committed to ensuring that the work of Alfonso Carboner was completed. He was a true, devout believer. The other three were very unsure, although each of them knew they had no alternative but to comply. They had come too far and after all they did believe in the vision. They were all a little uncertain about directly killing other people. They believed this was to be God's work. Developing a virus was easy but it was God who chose between the good and bad people, who would live and die. Surely it was not for them to decide. They were very confused by this new reality. Brother Xavi sensed their mood.

'I sense your concerns but I also sense your optimism. Let us grow your optimism and squash your concerns. We all know the right way to go. God is on our side. This will be God's work, remember, we are just his servants.'

He felt his words and his calming presence had helped. He looked at them all. They were looking better. They were looking more committed.

'Remember God is our guidance. Our Lord needs our help. Are we to fail him at this late stage? Is the devil going to win by breeding uncertainty and doubt amongst us? I say no, never!' he paused, breathless with emotion. He scoured his colleagues beckoning them to support him.

Reason to Believe

'What do you all say?'

The others all looked at him with renewed vigour and led forcibly by Father Jordi chanted loudly, 'God is our guide. God is our guide'.

The mood had improved and Brother Xavi seized on it.

'We need to act quickly Brothers. We need to be ruthless. There can be no room for doubt. Remember doubt is a seed sown by the devil.'

The body language of the Brothers now reflected unity and a preparedness to do what was necessary. Xavi continued, 'The toxicant is nearly ready but the antidote is not quite ready. We need to keep working on these. It will take us a few more weeks. In the meantime we need to ensure that Albert and his female supporters do not succeed in their quest.'

'What do you want us to do?' asked an eager reinvigorated Ramon.

'We need to get rid of him. He is the only danger. He needs to die,' said Brother Xavi coldly.

Jorge looked at Xavi with steel in his eyes.

'I will do it. He never liked me and I never liked him. It would be a pleasure to do God's work.'

The others all nodded in agreement. The brotherhood was re-established and the mission was back on track. Brother Xavi nodded his contentment, 'OK. That is good. Victor and Ramon you two continue your work on the antidote, Father Jordi and I will complete the virus and you, Jorge, will rid the world of the evil Albert. As a chemist I suggest you find a quick and easy method of control!' The chill in Brother Xavi's voice froze the dank atmosphere of the ancient room.

Reason to Believe

20

The phone tone was definitely Montse's. It was the Gypsy Kings hit single from the 1980's 'La Bamba'. Christy ignored the sound although Montse reacted and pulled the phone from out of her handbag. She flicked open her mobile and listened. As she did so her face dropped in shock.

'No, no. noooooo!'

'What's wrong?' asked Christy concerned.

'Nooooo Papa. Papa is dead. Papa is dead,' she repeated.

Christy looked at her sister and reached out for her before they both crumpled to the floor. They were on their knees facing each other with Montse still listening to the mobile glued to her ear.

'What happened Florita? Tell me, tell me!'

Steve Kenning

Christy moved her head towards the earpiece to hear the reply. She could hear Florita's voice, as composed and as matter of fact as ever.

'Well, Vittoria went round to see if Papa was OK this morning and when she got to his apartment she found him dead in bed. She became very hysterical as you can imagine. It took her about ten minutes to do anything. Then she phoned Adrianna who instantly phoned me. I got there as soon as I could and called the police. Listen Montse...,' Florita paused briefly '...There is no doubt he was murdered.'

'Oh no,' squealed Montse.

'Yes,' continued Florita with a hard edge to her voice, 'I think this whole business Papa was involved in, and has now dragged us all into, is very serious and could end in more deaths if we are all not very careful. We need to work on this together, safety in numbers. I am going to help you three. I am worried.'

'Are you sure?' replied Montse. She paused for thought for a few seconds, 'Papa is dead but we need to stop this virus. Can you spare the time?'

'Yes, I'm coming. It looks like Papa was suffocated. The room was a right mess. Not Papa's style at all. Whoever killed him was looking for things in the room or maybe it was meant to look like a burglary,' continued Florita.

Reason to Believe

'You seem very together as usual Florita. Your strength is a great help,' added Montse truthfully.

'You know me Montse, I am the least emotional person you know. I will shed a few tears at some time and I will miss Papa, but he was old. I would miss you three far more if you were killed. I may seem harsh with my words but that is the truth. Anyway, I cannot stand anymore of Vittoria's wailing. Adrianna is doing a great job managing her. Where are you?' questioned Adrianna.

'We need to see Papa,' replied Montse.

'No you don't,' answered Florita, 'Whatever he got Albert involved in is extremely serious and is far more important than seeing the dead body of your father. That can wait. He will sit in the morgue until we say otherwise. Whatever you need to do must be done quickly, where are you?' Florita repeated.

Montse looked at Christy who had heard everything. With their eyes they both acknowledged the sense of urgency in their sister's words.

'Listen Florita you are right. You need to be part of what we are doing. We are in the library on Calle de Wellington but we need to move on. We will meet you in twenty minutes in the Café del Born. Yes?' relayed Montse.

'I'm on my way,' replied Florita.

Steve Kenning

Christy and Montse just looked at each other for a few minutes. Christy spoke first, 'If they have killed Papa they could kill us. What have we got involved in Montse?'

Her sister looked at her with calming but steely eyes.

'I don't really care what all this is about but I do know that Papa was basically a good man despite this mess he had obviously got himself involved in. No-one is going to get away with killing Papa.'

'Yes but isn't this a job for the police. It's all getting a little too heavy. I'm worried that we can handle these people Montse,' replied Christy.

Montse sensed her sisters concern and realised she alone couldn't convince her that they had no option but to resolve this whole situation. She needed her husbands help, she urged her sister, 'Come on let's find Albert and get ourselves to Café del Born,' she said.

Twenty minutes later the three of them were sitting around a table in the high ceilinged popular meeting place in the trendy Born area of Barcelona known as Café del Born. Albert really liked the place, as it was full of young and old professionals just passing the time of day either at their computers or with their friends or associates. The mood of this particular small party was very maudlin and serious. The three of them stared at their café cortados and hardly spoke.

Reason to Believe

Some minutes later their sister Florita strolled in with a big smile on her face. Alongside her small frame was a huge man dressed all in black.

'Hi everyone, let me introduce you to Detective Will Ferran, an old friend of mine,' stated Florita.

Detective Will Ferran looked anything like a detective. He was in his late forties and looked like a faded rock star, long black hair, velvet suit and slim, attractive features, calm and charismatic.

'Hello, nice to meet you all,' he said to the semi-stunned group. Florita and the Detective sat down and ordered a couple of coffees. The others stared with a sense of vacancy on their expressions.

Montse was the first to say anything.

'What? Florita, what is going on? Who is this man?'

'Detective Will Ferran,' repeated the detective holding out his hand towards Montse in an attempt to greet her.

'Yes, but why are you here?' stuttered Montse.

'To help you,' answered the detective.

Montse looked accusingly at her younger sister, 'Florita what right did you have to involve the police without talking to us?'

Florita was having none of her elder sister's attitude, 'Look Montse, I know it is a surprise but when I saw Papa's dead body it just didn't look right. I have known Will for years, so I gave him a call. He was at Papa's apartment in minutes and confirmed what I thought. It was Will that raised the suffocation theory. We are looking at a murder. I had to involve the police. Anyway I thought he would be a useful ally with our investigations.'

There was silence in the room. Albert, quite composed about the death of his father-in-law, tried to relax the developing mood, 'Detective Ferran. Do you know the possible background to Senor Moncada's death? What exactly has Florita told you about the circumstances?'

Detective Ferran positioned his huge, six foot five inch frame more comfortably on his wooden chair before replying, 'Well as Florita said, we are old acquaintances from many years ago. She called me when she suspected foul play with your father. She was right. He was murdered. Then she told me about what you three were up to. I have to say that the intelligence units of the Mossos d'Esquadra had heard rumblings of activities of this group but there have been no real leads or evidence of wrongdoing. The common view is that they were generally a group of fairly harmless religious fanatics. This is obviously not the case if they are, as we presume, implicated in the death of Senor Moncada. So Albert, I am naturally very interested in what you are doing.'

Albert was a little surprised by the force of the reply. He was immediately impressed by the strength and confidence of the detective.

Reason to Believe

'What if we want to handle this ourselves?'

'No chance,' quickly interjected Ferran, 'This appears to be a really serious situation. You can save the world Albert, in fact it appears that only you can, but I can assure you at some point you will need our help.'

Albert was unusually flustered. Montse calmly put her hand on her husbands shoulder, 'Detective Ferran, we do need your help but you also need to protect us.'

Ferran stared Montse straight into her eyes, 'We will totally protect you. The problem we have is this. The Credo of Dulcinia, or whatever they are called, do appear to be quite clever and they are fanatical. They have obviously been watching you and they seem to know what your father has told you. They have moved their operation from the Ciutat Vella already. We have no idea where they are at they moment. All we know is that there are five of them. We have their descriptions and every Mossos officer is looking for them, but you will appreciate with several hundred thousand tourists in the city it is virtually impossible to find them. You three are our best course of action. We need to discuss how we can best help you?'

'Do you really believe all this Millenarium stuff detective?' asked Christy.

'Of course, Florita told me what Albert had seen and also there was your fathers letter.'

'A letter?' queried Montse.

Florita reacted, 'Yes, here it is. He knew he was going to be killed. We found this in his biscuit jar. We all know that's where Papa keeps his.....sorry, kept his money. So we checked it to see if his money had been stolen. It hadn't but we found this letter in the jar.'

Florita took an envelope out of her handbag and put it on the table in front of them all.

'We have also checked out the Palau dels Marquesos de Llio and the house on Calle de Larc de Sant Vicence. We can't find a way into a secret room. We can't even find a secret room in the Palace, although we will keep trying. However, we have found evidence of recent chemical activity in Calle de Larc de Sant Vicence,' announced Detective Will Ferran.

21

The plan was clear. Kill Albert, complete the work on the virus and resolve the antidote. In respect of the first objective Jorge had been left to his own devices to achieve his target. His mission was straightforward. He had to rid the world of the devils agent Albert, the threat to the survival of the Millenarium. His task clearly fixed in his mind, Jorge walked purposefully along Via Laietana. He particularly disliked this part of Barcelona as it was always full of tourists, cheap shops and continuous traffic, but soon he was onto Urquiaona and across onto Calle Pau Claris. He was heading for Albert's office on Calle Dispacio in the optimistic hope that he was there. He had no plan, just the intense desire to kill his brother-in-law.

Steve Kenning

Jorge was surging determinedly along Pau Claris when a book caught his eye in the window of the Laie bookshop. He stopped suddenly and stared at the book. It had an unusual cover revealing an almost negative photograph of a Barceloneta street but in purple. Despite the unusual cover, it was the title that had grabbed his attention, 'La Hermandad del Noveno Noviembre'.

Jorge checked his steps and headed into the bookshop. Inside he picked up the book and read it's back cover. It appeared to be no more than a frivolous thriller based in Barcelona, although the title 'La Hermandad' had made him think. Was he just part of a brotherhood or was he really doing God's work? He had never really thought about why he was driven to do what he was doing other than simply to please his Lord. This sudden doubt worried him. He felt fine about killing for the God he loved, especially about killing Albert who had always represented the 'perfection' side of the family and yet represented evil in respect to his millenarian aims. Yet this book made him think and he doubted himself, something he had not done since he joined the Dulcinian Creed some ten years or more ago. Was he fulfilling God's work or was he merely part of a brotherhood intent on completing a mission? He hated terrorism and the book he had glanced at had made him think that perhaps he was nothing more than a religious terrorist. Jorge was an intelligent person and he had always been fully aware that

Reason to Believe

many people had strong views about something, usually something that was particularly important to them. So was he simply a fanatic? These thoughts unsettled him. He bought the book and went upstairs to the café and ordered café con leche. For several minutes he perused the book whilst he drank his coffee. At the end of his coffee he still wasn't sure. The book appeared to be a basic thriller yet there was an edge to it that he didn't usually find in the mass-produced formula thrillers he sometimes read. As he glanced through the book quickly one paragraph jumped out at him:

'People come together, as a group for a wide variety of reasons. Sometimes they are forced together, sometimes it is by circumstance, but often it is by choice. Humans are inherently social animals and they feel happier, more secure and stronger in a group than they do individually. A brotherhood can be defined in several ways: It can be seen as the state or relationship of being brothers, or as a fellowship. A really precise definition is an association of men, such as a fraternity or union, united for common purposes.'

These words left him confused. Was he on a mission from God or on a mission to simply fulfil the needs of his brotherhood?

Steve Kenning

As he sat over the remnants of his coffee deeply disturbed by his discovery his phone rang. He pulled his mobile out of his pocket and listened.

'Jorge. Where are you? Have you found him yet?'

'Brother Xavi?' questioned Jorge.

'Yes it is I. I am concerned for our mission. Do you need help?'

'No I am fine. I am just deciding on the best approach. I want to make sure that my actions are appropriate. I don't think he is at work today anyway. The last time I saw him was at the library near the Ciuatadella Parc. I will find him, rest assured,' replied Jorge.

'Good. I was worried about you Jorge. You are very important to our mission. Let me know if you need our support. Good luck,' countered Xavi.

'I am fine. Thank you for your support. I will do what is right,' concluded Jorge. The phone rang dead. Jorge stared into his coffee. He didn't know in his own mind what was right. Although he knew Brother Xavi had a very clear view of the situation in his head and Jorge did not want to let him or his Lord down.

Reason to Believe

22

Ferran took control. He was an impressive character. His huge frame exuded confidence and capability. All three of them, Albert, Montse and Christy liked him instantly. He gave them confidence and credibility. Christy fell in love with him. She whispered to Montse, 'Who is this guy? He is gorgeous and so cool.'

Then Ferran spoke and the three women hung on his every word, Albert too was captivated by the detective's confidence.

'From what you have all told me there are several things we need to do: Albert you need to find this diary of Alfonso Carboner. I don't think the words you have found are the words you need to destroy the orb. It is all too easy, there

Steve Kenning

has to be more. The 'Divine Comedy' is too common a poem. I even learnt it at school heaven forbid, so there has to be more. What you have found is an easy diversion. The Dulcinians will be pleased with what you have found out. However, I believe there is much more, I am convinced. You also need to visit the village in the Pyrenees where Fra Dolcino is supposed to be buried and then to think again, is the information right, is it the right place? I am not convinced. There are plenty of false trails have been laid by supporters of these creeds. In ancient days to prevent the graves of the rich and important being ransacked for valuables and money, they often designated alternative graves or the real gravestone bore the name of another person.'

Albert jumped in to the conversation at this point, 'Yes, I agree, that is probably why Senor Moncada said that in his vision he didn't see us at the expected grave. He thought it was at a grave belonging to a follower of Fra Dolcino, although from what you say Ferran, it may actually be his real grave.'

Ferran acknowledged Albert's input with a supportive nod before continuing.

'Also, what does it say in this diary of Alfonso Carboner? It seems that the transect from his diary was put onto the internet by an unofficial follower. It was, I think, a mistake. I think that if you can find that diary you may find the

Reason to Believe

answer. Albert if you can find that diary then I believe you will save the world. The diary will have the answers to all your questions.'

Detective Will Ferran was confident in his words. He gave the impression that he wasn't scared by anything. Life in his beloved city of Barcelona was tough but his job was to make the place better. This was just another case, however unusual.

Albert took the lead following the words of this confident and educated detective.

'OK Ferran, I have heard of you and we have crossed swords in court, as you know, but despite that I do like your integrity. You have an excellent reputation for doing the right thing. For that alone I respect you immensely.'

Ferran looked a little surprised by Albert's words.

'But, you do not know everything. This is a family affair and it will remain so. I would appreciate it if you could investigate this Dulcinian creed and stop their activities. However, in the meantime the Moncada and Puigcada families will pursue their natural inclination to revenge Senor Moncada's death and to put an end to the supposed threat to the world. We would prefer to be allowed to work things out in our own way. Your support may be needed but only when we call for it,' stated a confident Albert.

Montse, Christy, Florita and Ferran all looked at Albert with their mouths open. That had been quite a speech for someone under some pressure. Montse reacted by hugging Albert's arm and Christy stroked Ferran's leg, much to his alarm. Ferran and Florita looked at each other with Ferran's eyes saying 'what have you got me into?'

Ferran tried to ignore Christy's advances and instead reacted to Albert's words.

'I have to say Albert that you are one of the coolest guys I have ever worked with. In court I have always thought of you as just another boring lawyer just doing your job. But, hey, with this situation you are acting really sensibly with clear thinking and with a strong element of cool. Go with what you are thinking but just keep me informed and ask for help when you need it,' stated the detective.

'What?' queried Florita.

'Ferran, are you mad? He is a company lawyer, he is not used to dealing with death threats,' interjected Florita.

Montse stood up and supported her husband.

'Florita, you are wrong, I know that Albert knows what to do. We need to trust and believe in him'

The group was silenced at this point. No one wanted an argument. Albert stared respectfully at Ferran and spoke.

'I do know what to do.'

'I also know, so call me if you need help,' responded Ferran.

'I will,' replied Albert.

Reason to Believe

23

The letter written by Senor Moncada, the father of Montse, Christy, Florita, Adrianna and Vittoria and the father in law of Albert, rested on the table in front of them. They were all sat silently looking at it. Then Florita jumped in with a statement, 'I know what it says. Shall I read it to you all?'

Before they had time to respond she had picked up the letter and pulled out the hand written note from inside the envelope. She held the letter in front of her and slowly began to read:

'My dearest children, my beautiful girls.

When you read this letter, I will be dead. Please do not grieve too much for me, just remember the good life we all enjoyed together. I am pleased to be joining your mother in heaven, at least, if God forgives my sins.

As you now know, I have recently developed this dreadful quality that gives me the ability to see what might or might not happen in the future. I am told it is called presience. I have seen my fate and I feel powerless to stop it and too weak and tired to avoid it. I have seen Brother Xavi, one of my former brothers in the Utilitarian Dulcinian Creed, come into my home and suffocate my sleeping body with a pillow. Yes, I could have stayed with one of you and I could have told the police, but that would simply have put off the inevitable. I sense that my time has come.

I am scared. Throughout my life I have expected that one day I would meet my Lord in heaven. Now though, because of what I have helped start, I am not sure if this will happen. I believe in the Day of Judgement and I hope that my recent actions to remedy this whole nightmare situation that I have helped create will stand me in good stead. I hope that when the last pages of the book of my life are read at the gates of St Peter they will reflect well on me.

I am sorry I involved you all in this dreadful situation, but, in the end, to save my soul and the world, I had no real option. I know Albert will succeed although he will need your assistance. I realised today that there is more that I know that might help you in your quest. I remembered

Reason to Believe

something about the source of our misdemeanours, the man known as Alfonso Carboner. I recalled that he was a great reader, but also a writer. He wrote many books about his philosophy. These might have some kind of important reference in them that will help you. There is a place where you may find some of these books. Search them out, as I am sure they will help you in your quest. The place you will have success at, I am sure, is an antique bookshop on the Placa dels Peixos. Ask for an Enrique Girondel. Albert's grandfather was a good friend of his.

My time is near, I feel happy about it but unsure about where it will lead. My presient ability has provided me with two visions of your futures. If Albert succeeds then we can forget the dreadful scenario facing the world, if this happens then I have seen a good life for you all. I pray to our Lord that he does. I love you all.

Papa.

Florita stopped reading and raised her head. Christy and Montse were sobbing. Albert put one arm around each of their shoulders to comfort them. Albert and Florita acknowledged each other with their eyes accepting that it was best to let the two sisters grieve for a few minutes. Eventually, Montse recovered her composure and wiped her eyes with a paper handkerchief.

Steve Kenning

'Ok, that's that.'

She stood up and looked at the ceiling of Café del Born. Then she said, 'Papa I love you and I will miss you forever but I will grieve more for you at your funeral. I know you will agree that now we must get on with our task.'

Montse looked determined and ready for action. She was a strong and resilient person, determined to achieve their aim. At the same time Christy stood up and moved towards the toilets without a word, keen to repair her make-up. Albert paid the bill and they were ready to go.

Reason to Believe

24

The two men were sitting in the sunshine on two aluminium chairs central to an array of about twenty or so that surrounded the little wooden shack that acted as a café in the centre of the Estacio Parc de Nord. The sun glistened off the large blue ceramic sculpture that was angled across the grass some hundred metres in front of where the men sat.

'Tell me what you are thinking,' asked the bearded older man. He looked carefully at the young dark haired, black bearded young man in front of him. The older mans eyes penetrated his colleagues through thin rimmed glasses. The younger man wriggled in his seat. Uncomfortable with this attention he seemed nervous and agitated. The older man stroked his neatly cropped beard with his right hand.

'You look concerned Jorge,' continued the older man.

Jorge sat on his hands nervously, trying to relax himself.

'I want to kill him, but I don't know how to or if I have the mental strength.'

The older man said nothing for a moment before quietly and calmly replying.

'Jorge, I expected as much. That is why I am here to offer you support. Remember that you have nothing to fear. You are doing God's work. It is work to save the Millenarium. It is to save the world from the evil greed that is destroying this paradise. You must remember that you will be welcomed into the kingdom of heaven for your deeds.'

Jorge didn't look anymore relieved by the words of Brother Xavi.

'I know that Father Jordi and you believe that I believe in our work. It's just that I have never killed before and I am afraid. I will do it though. I will,' replied Jorge, as if trying to convince himself. His forehead had beads of sweat on it and he appeared to be a little out of control.

'Calm down Jorge,' said Brother Xavi, 'I will help you. Together we will resolve this problem. We need to be clear about how to achieve this and where to do it. It is best to make it look an accident. I assure you that you will not feel anything but pleasure when we have achieved our aim.'

Reason to Believe

Jorge relaxed a little and put his hands in front of him onto the table. He looked at Brother Xavi searching for help and guidance.

'How should we do it?'

Brother Xavi had it all worked out.

'We will wait for them to start to head towards the hidden grave. If we take our time we may find that they fail to even reach it. They have much to discover and it is a long way from here. We will watch them carefully. I am sure they will find its origin. Some years ago one of our creed mistakenly tried to tell the world about what we were doing by publishing the diary of the great Alfonso Carboner on the internet.'

Jorge looked shocked, 'Why?'

'He thought that by opening up to the world the thoughts of a great philosopher, Alfonso Carboner, they would realise just how foolish they were being in leading their material driven, selfish lives. Unfortunately, instead it merely alerted certain people to the fact that we, the Dulcinian Utilitarian Creed, existed and that we had a plan of action. Since then, through a lot of hard work and careful planning we have managed to keep the police away from us,' replied Brother Xavi.

'Who was it?' asked Jorge.

'You may remember a young recruit, Phillipe, he was a French Catalan,' he paused, 'He left us.'

Steve Kenning

Jorge knew exactly what Brother Xavi meant. He felt chilled by the thoughts running through his head. Everything was confused in his mind. The work the creed was doing was so right and fully supported their Lord, but all these deaths, all this killing, seemed wrong. He tried not to reveal his thoughts to his elder.

'So where should we do it?' asked Jorge, returning to the original topic of conversation.

'We will tamper with their car on the way to the mountains. It will look like an accident,' said a cold faced Brother Xavi. He spoke with confidence, as he knew for a fact that this action would not be necessary as Father Jordi was already on a special mission for his Lord.

25

'The problem as I see it,' explained Albert to Christy, Montse and Florita, as they sat at the table at the café in front on the Gaudi inspired fountain in the Ciutadella Parc.

'Is that the people we are dealing with are religious fanatics inspired by political idealism. They are deeply religious people who believe that Hitler was on the right track with his idea of the Third Reich. This view has become even more cemented in their belief systems today as they can see evidence of our planet falling apart, whilst at the same time religious observance is at an all time low. They probably believe that as humans appear to be rejecting their role as stewards of the planet and destroying the earth, then God needs to re-establish his will. They undoubtedly feel there is a need for strong moral guidance and the creation of a safe whole new world.'

The sisters had no argument with Albert's reasoning. They agreed with his sentiments. The only real question on their minds was spoken by Christy, 'Yeah Albert I think we all agree with your theory but the big issue is, how do we stop this fanaticism?'

Fifteen minutes later and the four of them had traversed a good two miles of the city on the relatively free transport system provided through the 'bicing' bikes made available for the use of the citizens of Barcelona. They were on the trail of the diary of Alfonso Carboner. The snapshot of his diary that Christy had picked up off the internet had provided them with an unexpected lead. On reading Senor Moncada's letter to his daughters Albert had recalled a friend of his grandfathers who had known everything about and everyone who had lived in the old city. Their plan was to ask this man about the diary. Enrique Girondel was a man of his word and someone his grandfather had trusted implicitly.

Albert remembered visiting Enrique ten years or so ago to invite him to his grandfathers funeral. He had a good memory for places, although the workplace of Enrique Girondel would be hard to forget. His bookshop was in a building that was extremely grand, although not imposing, as it was easy to walk past it without really noticing it. It was

Reason to Believe

not on any of the mainstream routes of the city, but just off one of the main shopping streets of the city. The Casa Sacerdotal de Barcelona, as the building was called, was on Placa dels Peixos and part of the building was given over to the Libreria Balmes. Enrique was an antique book collector and his own library was just to the left of the Libreria Balmes bookshop. The entrance to his library was through an intricately iron sculptured adorned doorway, which was elaborate for effect and prestige. It said to the observer that they were entering somewhere different and unique. Albert's memories reminded him that anyone passing through the doorway would not have been disappointed. He stood in the street marveling at the doorway before pressing the top buzzer.

'Hello, who is it?' said an anonymous voice.

'It is Albert Roig. I'm looking for Enrique Girondel, he was a good friend of my grandfather.'

There was a brief pause. Then the iron-adorned door swung inwards. Standing inside a large hallway was a small man, well into old age. He wore a grey shirt buttoned up to the top and a grey v-kneck, sleeveless jumper. He held his arms out and welcomed Albert.

'Albert! Albert! I do so miss your grandfather.'

The old man hugged Albert fondly.

'Tell me, how are you?'

Then he noticed the three women.

Steve Kenning

'And who are these beautiful women?'

Before waiting for an answer he answered his own question, 'Your daughters?' smiled the old man.

Albert laughed, 'Grandfather always said that you had the words to flatter any woman. No, they are not my daughters. This is my wife Montse and her two sisters Christy and Florita.'

'I am very pleased to meet you all,' he announced graciously before pausing and looking at them questioningly. He continued, 'Now I am sure this is not a social visit, I can sense a tense mood amongst you all,' not waiting for a response he welcomed them in, 'Please come inside. I have coffee ready made.'

The four of them followed the old man into the building. The inside of the library bookshop was a large stone arched hallway covered with old manuscripts in heavy wooden frames. At the end of the hallway were a few stone steps that led into a huge library of books. Enrique's desk was at the back of the room in front of a large stone edged window. There were several brown leather armchairs littered around the room. The library was very tidy and well ordered.

'My life's work,' announced Enrique gesturing at the thousands of books that filled the shelves of the library.

'Are you a specialist collector?' enquired Florita.

'Not at all, unless you consider Catalan to be of special interest. I have a copy of virtually every published book in

Reason to Believe

the Catalan language. Many are not originals. I make a lot of money from selling the originals but I always make a good copy. Through there,' he pointed towards the rear of the room towards a secondary space, 'I have an old printing press, photocopiers, computers, binding machines and more. I am an expert at copying books,' he said proudly pointing towards a small door at the end of a huge bookcase.

'How do you cope with the volume of books produced now?' asked Albert.

'Ahhh, you were always very sharp Albert. When I said I have a copy of every book written in Catalan I should have qualified myself by saying 'up until the year 2000'. I decided that age was catching up with me and I decided to semi-retire then. The year 2000 was my Millenarium, my final year. I am eighty-six years old and still trading my books however. I love my work.'

The old man gestured them to sit down, dashed into the back room and suddenly returned with a pot of hot coffee in his hand. He poured them each a cup without asking their preference.

'Here, you all look like you need a cup of strong coffee. Drink it black. It will do you good,' Enrique instructed.

He sat down behind his desk.

'Now then, tell me how I can help you.

26

'Pro senior EGO mos tribuo meus animus.

Pro senior EGO mos tribuo meus animus.

Pro senior EGO mos tribuo meus animus,' he repeated silently under his breath, time and time again. By now it was a mantra, rhythmic and hypnotic. His head rocked slowly backwards and fore-wards, almost touching the ground in front of him. He had been on his knees, prostrate for over an hour, looking for peace of mind. This was his method of contacting his Lord. First came the deep concentration in silence that brought about the state of

Reason to Believe

meditation, then the chanting, before finally a flash of a vision. This is the way his Lord had helped guide him through his life for the past forty-five years.

'Pro senior EGO mos tribuo meus animus,' he continued. His heavy black woollen cloak spread out around him like a sea of crumpled waves across the stony floor. The beads of sweat littering his forehead were slowly turning into rivulets of clear liquid racing down his face before dripping to the floor. He was building up into a frenzy, his temperature rising in stark contrast to the atmosphere of the large, cold room he had entered alone earlier that evening. His thick, roughly shorn, black haired head, moved increasingly quickly as he built the tempo.

'Pro senior EGO mos tribuo meus animus.'

'Pro senior EGO mos tribuo meus animus.'

'Pro senior EGO mos tribuo meus animus.'

He was almost shouting but breathless as he rocked manically. Then the climax came unannounced and dynamically. As he rocked forward for the umpteenth time his body went into a spasm sending him reeling across the cold, dark stone.

'Aaaargh! Yes, my Lord,' he shrieked, 'I hear you! I hear you,' he continued triumphantly.

Then it was all over. Silence enveloped every crevice of the high ceilinged, dark room. A candle flickered on a table some twenty metres away from the crumpled heap of a man.

Steve Kenning

Dim light shone in from street lights through a couple of dirt lined windows. He was alone.

He was not a young man, far from it, and the damage done to his body following the exertion of the past minutes had to be repaired. The silent heaving of his chest as he lay spread-eagled on his back gradually eased. The sweat that had so recently flooded out of his pores quickly ran dry in the cold environment. His eyes opened and stared towards an imaginary heaven. A slight smile ran across his face.

'Pro senior EGO mos tribuo meus animus. For the Lord I will give my soul,' he uttered quietly to himself, 'I am you servant.'

He lay there as he had fallen, silently running through the vision that had entered his mind at the point of climax. He was looking for meaning to what he had seen. What was his Lord telling him? Time meant nothing to him and he lay there prone for a long time. At last he spoke to himself again.

'It is clear my Lord. I understand your message. I know what you expect me, your mere servant, to do. I will not, I will never, deny your testament.'

Then he was back to some kind of normality. As he sat up he wrapped his loose cloak around him for warmth as the sweat from his body had attracted the damp, cold air of the room. As he did so he shivered. Standing up was a slow process as he suddenly felt very tired. He rose up on one

Reason to Believe

knee and used the wall of the room to support the difficult climb to his feet. He peered around the vast room, quickly surveying the huge flagstones that covered the floor and the bare stone walls. He walked slowly over to the candle as if he was barely able to walk. He extinguished the flame with his fingers and eased his way across the dark room to the door. Within seconds he was gone into the night. The work of his Lord beckoned.

27

The coffee was good, very good, so good that the four visitors to Enrique Girondel's bookshop momentarily forget why they were there. As they sat around the mahogany red rectangular table in the rear office of the library, Enrique sat patiently and enjoyed the sight of his visitors delight in the quality of his coffee. He loved quality and was proud of everything he did, including making coffee.

Albert was half way down his cup of heavy black coffee when he realised where he was.

'Oh, Enrique! I am sorry. Here we are wasting your time.'

'Relax, young Albert. Enjoy the moment. I have all the time in the world,' replied a content Enrique.

Reason to Believe

'Yes, Enrique, I remember the hours I spent here in your bookshop reading whilst you and grandfather discussed everything and put the wrongs of the world right.'

Enrique smiled recalling fond memories, 'Albert, your grandfather was one of the most moral men I have ever known. He was always worth talking to.'

Albert smiled too recalling what seemed to be blissful days.

'Enrique. Unfortunately we really are in a hurry. We have to find out as much information about a character called Alfonso Carboner as possible and we do not have much time.'

His voice was urgent and troubled.

'I sense a problem Albert. Do you want to share it with me?' quizzed Enrique. Albert looked at the three women for any kind of support. Montse shook her head. Albert thought for a moment and considered her to be right. It was too dangerous to involve this old man in their situation.

'I think it is too complex and too dangerous to tell you Enrique. Let me just say that if we find what we are looking for then we could save lives,' responded Albert.

Enrique looked Albert in the eyes for some time before he calmly continued.

'I trust you as if you were my son Albert. Perhaps one day you will visit me and tell me the full story, I would like that.'

Albert nodded his agreement.

'Come on then, lets get to work,' said Enrique as he stood up and moved towards his desk at the edge of the room.

'The name you mentioned, I know the name 'Alfonso Carboner', I believe there are several entries by him in my library. I seem to remember it was all in the early nineties. Let me see,' as he spoke he opened up a huge ledger book which was his register of titles. He glanced at the others guessing their thoughts, 'Don't worry, I am slowly transferring all this onto computer, but for now I know my way around my record books much more easily than a hard drive,' he sniggered.

Albert, Montse, Christy and Florita all gradually stood up and surrounded Enrique at his large wooden desk. The ledger he was reading was leather bound and at least A3 in size. It looked like an ancient scripture. As Enrique turned the pages they could not help but notice the neatness and care of the black ink writing that covered the pages. Each item was coded and had links and notes written next to each.

'Look, 1993, I was right. Here it is: 'The diary of Alfonso Carboner'. Let me make a note of the location,' Enrique scribbled down a fee words on a pad of paper.

'The notes here say that he visited the library around the same time and purchased various items,' continued the old man, 'Lets look in this book to see what he bought.'

Reason to Believe

Enrique reached across the desk and picked up a smaller, but much thicker leather bound A4 ledger. He noticed them all looking at him and, as he placed the book on his lap turning the pages, he explained his actions.

'This is my visitor book. It goes back to 1961 when I took over this library from my Uncle Juan,' he paused thoughtfully then asked, 'Do you think I have repaid his faith in me? He gave me this treasury of history and culture on the express understanding that I would protect and further Catalan culture. How have I done?' he smiled knowing the answer.

'There is no other place like this in the world Enrique, this is unique, your uncle would be proud of you,' commented Albert.

'You are kind Albert, but yes, I am pleased. I have enjoyed my life and the knowledge I have gained from my books. Anyway, this ledger shows all visitors to the library since 1961. You would be surprised by some of the names.'

He flicked through the pages.

'Carlos Arias Navarro, Head of the Spanish State during Franco's time in 1975, not a nice man, said the hand written notes. I think he wanted to close me down as Catalan was outlawed but there was a great deal of resistance from other politicians and particularly the young King, Juan Carlos. He came too, but much later in the 1980's. Jordi Cruyff came also, he was learning to speak Catalan.'

Steve Kenning

Enrique was engrossed and taking a long time to find the information they were looking for, Albert interrupted him, 'So Enrique when did Alfonso Carboner visit?'

Enrique realised his ponderance and quickly found the page he had been looking for.

'Yes, here it is, Friday 16th April 1993. He arrived at 10.36 a.m and left exactly two hours later. Let me see.......what did he buy?'

The old man carefully read his meticulous notes. He looked up at his audience with a surprised look on his face and took a few seconds before speaking. They were expectantly waiting for his words.

'Eugene Carlos Claris, what a surprise. Yes, now I remember your Alfonso Carboner,' the old man smiled.

'What do you mean?' asked Montse.

'Well he was not what I had expected. I remember now that he unusually booked an appointment with me ahead of his visit and specifically asked that no-one else be present in the library. That was most unusual. However I agreed to meet him as he said he was a Catalan cleric. He arrived in full regalia, not just a monk's robes but almost as if he was a pontiff, but in colours and robes I did not recognise. Everything was laced in gold but the base colour was deep, blood red. He startled me when he arrived outside the library. I thought he must be an extremely important religious figure, although when I looked him up afterwards I

Reason to Believe

could find no mention of him. It was only later that I discovered that he led a little known order of the Church.'

Enrique continued to remember and gradually the images of the visit flooded back to him.

The old man was thinking hard, trying to remember the past and the character of Alfonso Carboner. He stood silently thinking for several moments. Then he stumbled backwards into the arms of Albert. Enrique looked troubled as he rested against Albert's chest. Albert helped him back to his feet but the old man was obviously troubled and resistant to revealing what exactly was concerning him.

'What is it Enrique? I can see that I have troubled you with my questions.'

Enrique cast Albert a closed look He obviously had remembered something he didn't want to share.

'What is it?' queried a persistent Albert.

Enrique moved over to his desk and sat in the leather backed high chair. He sat for a while looking at his knees, then he looked up at Albert, obviously having made a decision to speak.

'Albert, I can now understand why this man is so important to you. In all my years here I believe he was the most evil man I have ever met, yet I could not reconcile that feeling with his religion. His eyes were intense, so intense I couldn't look into them. I remember feeling that I might see the devil if I engaged his vision. He wanted me to have a copy of his diary and he wanted it to be made available to as many people as possible. I refused to publish it however and said I would only keep copies in the library,' said Enrique with a look of fear on his face.

'Why would you do that?' asked Albert.

'Publishing costs a great deal of money and I only published books that furthered Catalan culture. His diary certainly didn't do that.'

'Why didn't he get someone else to publish it?' asked Christy.

'I think he wanted his thoughts through his diary to seep out into Catalan society and a small, well-respected set up like mine would have done that. At that time there were few others with a reputation. He was cross when I refused but he still bought a couple of other books.'

'What did he buy?' asked Albert.

Enrique smiled again, 'You will not believe what he bought.'

He paused.

'Tell us!' the others cried out in frustration.

Laughing out loud Enrique just managed to tell them, 'Eugene Carlos Claris – 'The art of illusion'. He was a great Catalan magician, one of the first mentalists. I believe they made people believe they could see things. This guy had a real talent and was demonised by Franco. He ended his days in Montjuic. What a waste. Also, he took out two books

Reason to Believe

connected with devotion. Look, one book was called 'The disciples manual' written by someone by the name of Manuel Crespo, and the other was a Catalan translation of an American book, 'Leading the leadable' by Graham Seeger.'

The three women looked towards Albert, eyes wide in expectation.

Albert responded, 'Enrique, do you have all these books?'

Enrique laughed out loud.

'Albert, of course I do. Follow me.'

The old man stood up and walked over to the far side of the room. He beckoned them all to follow him. He opened a large wooden door and entered another room. They all gasped momentarily as the passed through into a cavernous room that was twice as high as the one they had just left. There was a mezzanine level skirting the whole of the room that was a big as a school hall. Every wall was full of books from floor to ceiling and in the centre of the room were tall bookshelves brimming with titles. It looked like a library from heaven. Nothing was out of place. Enrique strolled around the room looking. They followed him. Every now and then he selected a book from the shelves, looked at it, smiled and carried on. After five minutes he had four books in his hands. He looked at his small entourage.

'These are the books you need. Take them and find in them what you need to find.'

Steve Kenning

Enrique held the books out towards Albert.

'But, but, can we pay you for them? We are most grateful for your help,' responded Albert.

'No, no, no! I am pleased to help you Albert. Just return the books when you have finished and spend a morning revealing your story to me at some time in the future. That is all I ask,' replied Enrique.

They all sat looking at each other for a few seconds unsure as to the next move. Then Enrique took the lead.

'You have much to do. Go now and find out what you need to find out. I am sure these books will help you greatly. I am delighted to be of assistance.'

They all stood up together and Albert thanked his grandfather's old friend profusely.

'Enrique, it has been a delight to see you again and I thank you very much for your help. I will return very soon to tell you more. Thank you.'

Albert's words trailed after him as he left the room. The four of them hurried out of the library building and onto the street.

'Ok, where to know?' asked Florita.

'Somewhere quiet. There are four of us with four books to read,' responded Montse.

'Let's go back to Café del Born, it'll be quite quiet at this time of day and they have coffee on tap!' suggested Christy.

'Sounds good to me,' replied Albert.

Reason to Believe

28

His mind was very distracted and things appeared to be coming at him from every direction. He couldn't focus on the here and now, he was agitated and his thinking was disturbed.

'Sorry!' he muttered bumping into a passer by as he climbed the concrete steps out of Horta metro station. It was raining and the traffic was frantic. There were people everywhere. Jorge felt overwhelmed and confused. He looked a complete mess. The rain lashed his balding head, sweeping his dark hair in a variety of different directions. His clothes were dishevelled and increasingly damp as the torrential rain pounded the heaving streets.

Steve Kenning

He had been walking all day long. Until thirty minutes ago he had had no idea where he was. He had just roamed the city with his head down unaware of anything or anybody. His mind was tortured, unable to establish what was right and what was wrong. Jorge had two competing voices in his head, each questioning his motives and urging him to take action. He couldn't separate the voice of reason from the voice leading him straight to hell. He questioned his faith repeatedly during the day, calling on his Lord to support him in this hour of need and to offer him some kind of guidance. It was when he was sat huddled in a shop doorway on Diagonal, clutching his knees to his chin that he came back to some kind of reality. A pedestrian, mistaking him for a beggar, threw a two euro coin at him, hitting him on the nose. Jorge took it as a message from his Lord. It was a sign. He knew then what he had to do even if he had a feeling in the pit of his stomach that it was totally the wrong action.

'Victor! Victor!' he called as he opened the door to the small apartment in a non-descript block on an anonymous road in an un-distinct area on the outskirts of Barcelona. It was no more than ten years old and consisted of several small rooms all devoid of anything but an array of chemical equipment. This was the new laboratory.

'Jorge! We have been concerned about you.'

Reason to Believe

Victor peeled off his green rubber gloves and walked across to the pathetic looking Jorge and hugged him.

'Where have you been?'

Jorge slumped backwards, propping himself up against the wall. As he did so he glanced at the pristinely dressed Ramon, resplendent in red tie and black suit, standing behind a table littered with chemical activity. Ramon carried on with his work but cast a disapproving eye on Jorge.

'You look like shit. We need your help. We are never going to make the deadline,' he scowled as he poured a yellow liquid into a crucible. Then he gruffly moved away and scurried into another room. Jorge let out a huge sigh and looked up at his good friend Victor.

'Here, sit with me,' he pleaded, signalling with his left hand a suitable spot next to him on the marble floor. Victor looked down at the sad sight of his lifelong friend. He slowly sat down next to him. Tears welled up in Jorge's eyes as he spoke quietly to Victor.

'I don't know what is going on Victor. I can't bring myself to do what we are doing anymore.'

Victor was a little surprised but gently placed his hand on Jorge's arm. He sighed.

'Everything we have worked for, all the sacrifices we have made, it has all been for our Lord Jorge. Remember we are simply fulfilling his mission. We are his disciples.'

Steve Kenning

'Yes but how is it right to kill? Making the virus seemed so easy. We would never see exactly who we are killing. But......But to kill in cold blood, to kill my brother in law. I cannot do it. I cannot do it,' reacted a troubled Jorge.

Victor looked at his friend with astonishment. He had never seen Jorge like this before. His friend appeared to be bereft of belief and Victor struggled to find words to counter the power of Jorge's conviction. Victor took a few moments to think about how best to approach this situation, before he replied.

'I can understand my friend. This is a bad time for you with everything that is happening in your life, especially with Vittoria leaving you....'

'It is nothing to do with her.' Jorge snapped in a loud and aggressive tone. He stood up incensed.

'I am telling you Victor this is wrong. We have to stop what we are doing or we will go to hell,' stated Jorge forcibly.

Ramon put his head around the door from the neighbouring room to hear more of the argument. Victor struggled to his feet and held Jorge by his arms.

'You can't mean what you are saying Jorge. You are suffering from stress. We have been working on this for years. It is your formula. Think about what you are saying,' Victor implored.

Reason to Believe

'I have been. I am ashamed. I am wrong. This has to stop.'

Ramon moved back out of sight having heard the thread of the conversation. Within minutes he was relaying what he had heard to Brother Xavi on his mobile.

'You were right Brother Xavi. Jorge is here and he wants to stop everything.'

Ramon listened carefully to the reply.

'OK, OK. Yes, I will do that.'

Ramon closed his phone and marched into the other room and stood alongside Jorge and Victor.

'Jorge, you need to go home and get some sleep. Let us, the three of us talk about this tomorrow. Tomorrow when you are thinking straight,' announced Ramon assertively.

Jorge looked at him surprised.

'No, I don't need to talk. I'm going to put a stop to this now.'

He moved towards the glass apparatus urgently. Ramon and Victor got to him first and grabbed his arms in an attempt to stop him reaching the experiment. They struggled with him, pulling him towards the doorway that led out of the apartment.

'No, stop! Stop! I must destroy this work. It is evil,' shouted an increasingly deranged Jorge.

'No, you need to leave now,' replied Ramon as the two men shoved Jorge out of the apartment into the hallway.

Steve Kenning

Jorge could do nothing to counter their aggression. He had no strength remaining all his energy was sapped. All he could do was just look at the two men with resignation. As he sat still on the apartment building hallway floor he uttered, 'I will stop this madness, I will.'

Ramon looked at the helpless figure in front of him with disdain. He spat at him.

'I am ashamed of you. We are doing our Lords work and you, in the face of the slightest retort from our enemy the devil, decide to stop everything. What is wrong with you? You deserve to die with the rest of the filth of this society.'

Jorge ignored the words of the arrogant Ramon, instead he looked at Victor who stood staring sympathetically at his old friend.

'This is wrong Victor. You know it. I have told Albert. I have sent him a note explaining it all,' paused Jorge hoping for a reaction. There was none.

'Well? What about you? Do you feel the same Victor?' questioned Ramon uneasy and worried that he may be outnumbered.

It took the big man a few seconds of thought to reply.

'Not at all, I have been worried about Jorge for some time. I think you need some help my friend,' turning towards Jorge, 'But not from me. We have work to do.'

Ramon smiled.

Reason to Believe

'Good, enjoy hell,' he said smirking at the wreckage of Jorge as he guided Victor back inside the apartment. The door slammed shut leaving Jorge crumpled on the floor in the centre of the hallway of the modern apartment block. He lay there for some time unaware of anything or anyone. Even a woman resident of the apartment block, who almost tripped over him, quickly negotiated his bodily mass and hurriedly finding her way into her apartment before firmly securing the door behind her. His body lay there on the hard tile floor with no one willing to take any responsibility. It was sometime before Jorge realised where he was and what situation he was in. He felt as if he had been dope and drugged. He had no idea of what had happened when he eventually came round. Jorge managed to focus. As he did so he saw a black figure looming above him. Eventually he focussed on a familiar figure, he realised it was Father Jordi. He was relieved. After his disorientation he saw a friendly figure coming to support him in a time of need.

'Hello, Father Jordi. Thank you for coming to help me. I'm sorry I have caused you a problem. I can't help feeling as I do. I hoped you would understand.'

Father Jordi stood astride Jorge with a caring but intense look on his face. His black priestly robes hung down loosely around his body. He was old, well into his sixties, but he was fit and lean. The look on his face was purposeful.

Steve Kenning

'Jorge, I do understand your predicament. Let me help you,' said the wise old Brother. Jorge reached out his arms to his colleague, expecting support. The huge priest took hold of Jorge's head gently in his enormous hands. Then, quickly and without a sound, Father Jordi quickly turned his hands. There was a crack and Jorge's body was instantly lifeless. The priest relaxed his iron grip on Jorge's head and let it drop gently onto the floor. He placed the palm of his hand on the dead mans head and silently said a prayer.

'Jorge, you were wrong, so wrong. There is only one way and that is the way of the Lord. I am so disappointed in you. I am sorry, as I liked you a great deal. However, the Lord's work must be done and we must rid the world of the weak. That is you Jorge. You are one of the weak.'

Jorge body lay slumped on the tiled floor. Father Jordi looked down at his inactive body.

'I know you have been betrayed in your thoughts my Brother and therefore I ask our Lord to forgive you and to help you pass into the Kingdom of God. I will pray for you.'

The huge man stood astride his victim and prayed again for a few minutes. It appeared that he was looking for strength and direction. Then, without any indication of his intention, he picked the body up off the floor, placed it over his shoulder and headed off back down the stairwell from where he had come. Nothing remained on the floor outside the apartment.

Reason to Believe

29

'This is really quite fascinating,' commented an enraptured Christy as she pored over one of the books her two sisters and brother in law had picked up from the antiquarian bookshop.

'Look at this!' she said not waiting for a reaction, 'It appears that there are aromas that can, in particular environments, induce instant hypnosis.'

'What rubbish are you reading?' scoffed a sceptical Florita, her nose deep inside one of the four books they had collected from Albert's fathers old friend Enrique. She was leaning back in her chair holding the book at forty-five degrees above her head. She was enthralled and didn't want to be disturbed by trivial anecdotes.

Steve Kenning

'This makes a lot of sense,' Christy said, 'This Alfonso Carboner put up quite a plausible manifesto for life. He manages to make, even atheistic me, understand how religion, history and the purity of the human spirit could be utilised to the benefit of mankind through a Millenarium.'

Albert looked up from his reading. He sipped his coffee before quipping towards Florita.

'Don't tell me that you have found the new way forward for your political life?'

Florita scowled towards Albert and continued reading. Peace had been restored.

The daylight was just disappearing and a couple of people sitting at the metal outdoor furniture on Calle Commercial outside Café del Born felt
the chill of the first evening air and
moved inside the high ceilinged building.
The long room was full of early evening
custom and the air was a mixture of pale, sparse, smoke and gentle conversation. The round wooden tables were littered with an array of coffees or beers. The clientele were busy gently chatting, reading or working their laptops. The atmosphere was relaxed and tranquil.

Sat at the back of the long room at a small round brown wood table the small assembled group of Roigs and Moncada's were oblivious to their environment, they were

Reason to Believe

fully engrossed in their research and the books in front of them, the books that were possibly last read by the infamous Alfonso Carboner some thirty years ago. Coffees became beers as the hours passed by and the four of them swopped books, read, re-read and commented on particular points of interest as they arose from their reading. Eventually deep into the evening Albert closed the fourth book he had skimmed with a relish. The others looked up from their reading and waited for the inevitable words he was about to speak.

'Well, really interesting don't you think? Tell me,' he paused, 'About the overriding impression resting in your minds? Imagine that you know nothing about this whole Millenarium plot, what do the books tell you?' Albert asked. The others closed their books and considered his point for a moment or two. As they did so he gathered the books together into the centre of the small table.

'We have read 'The Diary of Alfonso Carboner', 'The Art of Illusion' by Eugene Carlos Claris, 'The Disciples Manual' by Manuel Crespo, and 'Leading the Leadable' by Graham Seeger,' he paused and looked around the table at the others, 'Well what do you think, what have we learned?'

Christy was the first to respond to her brother-in-laws request.

'I have learnt a great deal, particularly about Alfonso Carboner. There is no doubt that he was a very clever man.

Steve Kenning

He was well read and his theories and ideals were very plausible,' everyone nodded as Christy spoke.

'We also now know for definite exactly where we have to go to in order to speak the words over the grave of Fra Dolcino. He mentions the place several times in his diary. It is the place we discovered earlier, the diary just confirms it in the high Pyrenees, a place called Pardines,' added Montse.

'We can now understand that he was serious about the need to re-establish the Millenarium and its basic philosophy of 'cleansing' the world of sinners. It is a surprisingly powerful argument he puts forward in his writing,' continued Christy.

'Yes, but don't you think the other books confirm why all this is so dangerous?' questioned Florita, always someone keen to find the weakness in a theory. The others listened with interest to her observation.

'The Utilitarian Dulcinian Creed set up by Alfonso Carboner was just like all these other wacko quasi religious movements and cults that emanated in the 1970's and 1980's. What he did quite simply was to 'con' people into following his ideas,' Florita adjusted her seating position as she realised she had the full attention of the others, 'It really is quite simple. First of all you need to have a believable religious theory purported by a charismatic leader, you attract a collection of people looking for something to

Reason to Believe

believe in and then you brainwash them so they become real disciples to the cause, willing to do anything to please their leader and achieve the personal goal which ultimately involves them being given, or so they are told, a prime position in the Kingdom of Heaven. Religions have worked this way for many centuries, they obviously still do today.'

Florita looked around at the faces of her sisters and Albert as they considered her words. They nodded, her words made sense.

'I tend to agree with you Florita,' stated Montse, 'But how did he do it? How did he get people to believe in his ideas, I mean it is a bit extreme to try to murder most of the world, how do you sell that to other people?'

'I really don't know. We all understand his philosophy and the power of it, but not one of us would join his Creed with a view to carrying out the required action. Perhaps he was simply massively charismatic, maybe it was through the power of personality,' suggested Florita.

Albert had listened quietly to the sisters' conversation.

'I think you are right Florita in your outline of events. I imagine that Alfonso Carboner was a powerful speaker and although he appears to have been quite diminutive in size, at least he looks small from the couple of photographs we have of him, he was a great observer and supporter of the tyrannical European leaders of the mid-nineteenth century. Leaders such as Hitler, Mussolini and Franco in particular, all of whom were small, powerful men. He obviously learned a great deal from observing and reading about these leaders.'

'Yes, Albert but it still doesn't explain the hold he has had on his followers, some of whom have been recruited after his death,' Florita argued back.

'Well, I was coming to that. Christy made me think earlier with her comment about hypnotic aroma. With this in mind I read the books on leading others and illusion with a particular interest. I believe Alfonso Carboner developed a strong psychological technique, as do many other 'cult' leaders, in order to transfix the support of others. Unusually though in order to totally commit them to his cause and beliefs, he achieved this without the use of fear, instead he developed a range of illusions that when enacted appeared as 'miracles'. In his diary he utilised the world 'miracles' on a regular basis and he mentions one or two that he himself performed to his followers. Do you recall in his diary the one about the time they witnessed the spirit of Fra Dolcino at his graveside?' Albert conveyed to the others.

'Yes, I read that too,' said Christy, 'I thought it was a bit creepy though.'

'Exactly,' continued Albert, 'Imagine seeing the founder of your creed, who had died several hundred years ago, rising from his grave and spouting his belief to you in some ancient Italian dialect? I'd either be spooked or enthralled.'

Reason to Believe

'Too right,' added Christy, 'I'd run a mile!'

'I also think it makes sense to assume that Alfonso Carboner almost certainly passed on his skills to others when he died,' revealed Albert.

'Why on earth would he do that?' questioned Montse strongly.

'In order to keep his dream of the return of the Millenarium alive,' responded her husband.

'Papa! You don't think Papa was involved in this do you?' asked Christy with a look of distaste on her face.

Albert took a little time to reply, taking into account the expectant look on the faces of the three sisters.

'I really don't know. If he was involved he was very clever at hiding his illusionist talents. To be perfectly honest, and you sisters will probably not want to hear this, if these skills of deception were shared with him, then we would have to question a lot of what he did and said over the years. As a politician I really don't think he would have got away with using such techniques, as he would have been caught out. So, my original gut feeling was that he was unaware of all this. However, as I have been talking, I remembered the orb he showed me, the orb that appeared to be floating inside the wall in the room in the old palace.'

Albert took a sip of his beer and deliberately allowed the sisters to reflect a little on what he had said. It was a difficult thing to tell them that the father they had revered was in fact a sham. A few minutes later he continued.

'When Detective Ferran eventually found the room, and I later returned to it also, there was no sign of how the orb could be anything other than a real vision. But, Christy your comment on the aromatic hypnosis must have been the answer. The room the orb was in was sealed with no windows or doors, so no draughts were present to remove an aroma or gas. I remember that the room did smell very strange, but at the time I took it to be incense of some kind. But...,' he paused, 'But then your father described the orb to me. He told me what I was seeing. Auto-suggestion I think it is called. So despite my original gut feeling, I think your Papa at the very least knew how to aromatically hypnotise. I can think of no other explanation for what I witnessed in the old room.'

The sisters sat there aghast just looking at each other hoping that everything they were hearing was untrue. This was something they really had not considered. Their beloved Papa could not possibly be involved in such deception, although it did make sense.

Christy stood up and leant her head against the wall of the café. She turned around to face the others.

'But if he did do what you say Albert, which I agree sounds like the most common explanation, he was only doing it to get you to act with him, to believe in what he was

Reason to Believe

telling you,' she commented trying to protect her memories of her father.

'I can't believe it,' said a mystified Montse, 'This means that everything could be a lie. He might not even be dead.'

'He is dead Montse,' Unfortunately we were all witnesses to his dead body at the morgue. I think this hypnotic drug is only effective for short periods, in very enclosed spaces and can only be effectively used to suggest one image at a time to the victim. I don't see how it could be used in a mortuary. Look at this.'

Albert picked up a book from the pile in the centre of the table. The book had a hard purple cover with the title ingrained into the front, 'The art of Illusion'. The authors' name, Eugene Carlos Claris, was stencilled onto the spine of the book. Albert flicked through the browned leaf thin pages looking for his reference.

'Here,' he pointed and the others crowded round him to look at the section in the old book.

'The art of imagery.

A magician is constantly looking for something to entrance his audience. The quest for a visual tool that will hold the audience in awe and encourage them to tell their friends to visit the show is perpetual. Recently, on my journeys to the outer streets of the city of Buenos Aires, the exotic city in Argentina, I came across a fanatical attraction for illusion. There I met many men who claimed to be illusionists, but every single one of them was no more than a showman to somebody with my sharply trained magician eyes. Then, just before I was due to travel to the United States, I witnessed a street performance by a man simply called Raoul. I was stunned by his performance on a street corner to an audience of ten men and a dog. At one point in his performance I am convinced he raised his whole body off the floor and 'levitated' for some two minutes or more. I could see no method to his trickery. Immediately afterwards I spoke to the man and he invited me to buy him a meal. This I willingly did and then and there we began a lifelong friendship. I cancelled my visit to the United States and spent the following month learning Raouls illusions. He became a good friend and often visited me at my home in Spain. Alas, he passed away several years ago.

Perhaps the greatest thing Raoul taught me was not a trick but it was about a plant. He introduced me to a wild plant, which looked like a general everyday weed, called 'Alfa Baum'. Amazingly this plant only grows in South America and only alongside watercourses. 'Alfabaum' is a green plant that when dried, turns grey. Then, when pummelled, it disintegrates into a fine dust. The dust looks as if it is very harmless, but I believe, if it is inhaled it becomes a very strong halluciagenic drug. Rauol was a drug user and a friend introduced him to the plant because

Reason to Believe

it was basically free. The impact of the drug on the human mind was always very short lived and so the plant never became a popular taste amongst the rich elite of the South American cities, instead it became a poor man's relief. Raoul was an infrequent user and one day, when sitting with a couple of friends who had recently inhaled 'Alfa Baum', he discovered that they were very suggestible, as if they were hypnotised. His friends were willing accomplices over the following weeks as he investigated the hypnotic and halluciagenic powers of the drug.

I used the drug extensively in later years to perform what would otherwise be impossible illusions.'

Albert stopped reading and the women around him silently sat back in their seats. Christy was the first to respond.

'Quite incredible Albert, I know drugs but I have never heard of this one. It can only mean that Papa fooled you into seeing the orb, it doesn't exist!'

'I think you are right Christy. I can think of no other explanation. We can probably prove it by getting Ferran's forensic team to look for traces of the drug in the room at the Palace where I saw the orb,' replied Albert.

'I can't believe that Papa would be so deceptive. Why? Why did he do it?' questioned Montse.

Steve Kenning

'That we might never know,' answered Albert, 'Although if we piece everything together I think we will be able to hazard a good guess at the possible reasons.

Reason to Believe

30

Detective Will Ferran was not someone to waste time. He was a man of action and instinct. His instinct was his life and the reason for his success. He knew his instinct was his strength and something he had to trust. The situation involving the Moncada family was unusual. Florita, who he had known for twenty or more years, had got him involved, but why was it that he had doubts and didn't trust most of what she had told him. Albert Roig was also someone whom he had known loosely for many years, and Ferran knew by experience and reputation that he was absolutely trustworthy. Why was it then that he had doubts? He was troubled by his thoughts.

Steve Kenning

His doubts surrounded the death of Senor Moncada. He had been suffocated by his thoughts of this there was no doubt. But what troubled Detective Ferrran were the circumstances. There was absolutely no sign of forced entry or even invited entry into the apartment where the old man's body was found. Senor Moncada had been found in his bed and he had obviously, from his prone position, not got out of his bed to allow anyone into his apartment. No widows or doors had been opened forcibly and there was no evidence of a key having been used in the lock for several hours. To Detective Ferran this had to mean that someone was already in the apartment when Senor Moncada returned home. Whoever it was killed him before letting themselves quietly out of the apartment. If this was the case it really had to be one of the family. The only fingerprints found inside the building belonged to the family.

He had thought long and hard about this theory. He just could not find a reason, other than for money and insurance in particular, why any off the immediate Moncada family would kill their Papa. His team had quickly investigated each of them in order to assess their financial situations and, although Florita's needs, with her political aspirations, were greatest, none showed a need to maximise an insurance claim from Senor Moncada's death. He was busy musing on this avenue of thought when he had had an idea. Footprints.

Reason to Believe

Ferran busied himself around the white suited police. He had sent the forensic team back to the old man's apartment to recorded footprints, something they hadn't done first time around. Using a new infra-red device they discovered something strange. Size eleven sandals were all over the place. The only men who had recently been in the apartment apart from forensics officers were Senor Moncada, who had size eight feet, and Albert Roig with size nines.

Detective Ferran built on this information in his mind and started to piece together the story the Moncada sisters and Albert Roig had given him. His senses told him that this was a big situation and that they were, after all in all likelihood, telling him the truth. When he had met them all earlier in the Cafe del Born he had given them moral support without commitment, but now he realised that what they had been saying was probably connected to some sort of truth. As soon as the size eleven footprints had been identified Ferran had put his team onto investigating the weird group of Millenarianists, particularly the Xavi character, he had heard his name mentioned before.

In a short space of time, Ferran's investigators had uncovered a great deal about this organisation fronted by Xavi Bosch, the Dulcinian Creed leader. Each member of the group was identified and appeared to be relatively harmless except for Xavi and a character called Father Jordi. It appeared that there had been a number of violent incidents

Steve Kenning

connected to nationalism and religious fanaticism concerning Xavi and Jordi over the past twenty-five years. Both, when investigated in the past, had been considered to be harmless and fanatical hence both had escaped any punitive treatment. However, Ferran had through his research also picked up on the influence in recent times of Alfonso Carboner and the aspect of Millenarianism. As he had been given more information about the organisation led by Carboner, the more concerned he had become. A further survey of the locations in the Ciutat Vella pointed out to him by Albert Roig were completed and Ferran had found some evidence, although limited but confirming the information he had been given, of the possible use of chemicals and other visual stimulants.

Detective Will Ferran sat and stared into his black espresso. It was his fifth of the day and it was only ten-thirty. He knew exactly who he had to target, and he also knew what this case as all about. His next move was to find the proof and to put a stop to a potential threat to the well-being of his city. He leaned back in his chair, looked towards two of his junior officers who were sitting casually at their desks and said sharply, 'OK! This is it. Pick up Xavi Bosch.'

Ferran stood up.

'Let's go.'

Reason to Believe

31

'My friend, my very good friend, do you remember what our beloved inspiration Alfonso Carboner said to us, it must be fifteen or more years back when we were in Montserrat?' Xavi uttered fondly.

'It was eighteen years and two months to the day my Lord. We were indeed at Montserrat,' stated a be-cloaked Father Jordi.

Brother Xavi looked at his long-time friend, the timeworn Father Jordi, and took him into his arms.

'We have been together for too long to fail our Lord and our leader, my friend. Do you remember what Alfonso said to us?' urged Xavi.

The black haired priest looked aghast for a moment as if he had forgotten everything their inspirational leader had taught them. Then he composed himself, he smiled and looked up at his master.

'Yes I do,' he said proudly, 'Yes, I do.'

'He told us that our roles in life. The purpose of the rest of our lives is to ensure that the Millenarium is successful. We have to rid this world of evil and ensure its rebirth. We were given a plan. We must make sure the plan is committed. He gave us a reason to believe.'

His smile was as wide as his face.

Brother Xavi looked at his be-cloaked colleague. He knew that with the commitment of his friend and loyal subject that they would be successful.

'Have all obstacles been overcome? Is our plan on schedule?' asked Xavi.

Father Jordi smiled.

'I have eliminated non-believers my Lord and there are our two fellow followers who are ensuring that the necessary chemical reaction of our strategy is in place. There are now four of us my Lord, but that is all.'

The two men looked at each other and glowed with satisfaction. They reached out and held each other. They were elated. Smiling, they knew they were making a success of their actions.

Reason to Believe

32

It was quite late when Albert rose from his bed. Montse was nowhere to be seen. He paced barefoot, wearing nothing apart from his striped bed trousers, into the kitchen. His eyes were almost closed yet he automatically opened the fridge door for a bottle of water. As he swigged water from the bottle he remembered vaguely Montse getting up to take the children round to Vittoria's. He would normally have gone with her but last night on their return from the Café del Born, he had continued reading the books relating to Alfonso Carboner, and thinking. He eventually went to bed at about five a.m.

Steve Kenning

As he paced slowly across the brown tiled floor back into the hallway that led to his bedroom, he noticed an envelope on the small shelf that rested above the radiator. This was where he and Montse put their unopened post. He picked it up and saw that it was addressed to him in scrawly, hurried handwriting. He didn't often get hand written notes to his home address. He was intrigued so he opened up the envelope and unfolded the piece of paper that was inside it.

'Dear Albert,

This must not only be a strange thing for you to read, it must also be an essential thing for you to read. Please do not throw this letter away. Please continue to read and to absorb my thoughts.

I know that you and I have never seen eye to eye and that you believe I have badly treated your sister in law, Vittoria. I accept that perhaps I have always been a little distracted and misguided by my religious beliefs. This is because I am a Christian and I believe in God. However, I also believe in the Millenarian and that our present society is corrupt and, frankly, godless beyond redemption. Something has to be done to save humanity. I thought the best way was to punish the unbelievers and to create a new religious, principled, God loving society from the survivors. This, I now realise is not the right, God loving, way to deal

Reason to Believe

with the problem. My colleagues believe otherwise, but as I feel it is wrong to deliberately kill anyone, I feel that I cannot go through with the programme.

You, despite our distance and unfriendliness, I trust. I have always had a dislike for you. This is because you have a kind of godliness about you, you are blessed and serene, yet you do not believe in God and you are very open about it. This makes me question my beliefs. However, I trust you. You are either, misguided and unaware of the God in your life, or it is me that is besotted with something that does not exist. Regardless, I have decided to entrust you with the information that will end this nightmare of the Millenarium. I do believe in it, but not in the methods being adopted by my particular religious group. I believe the Millenarium will still happen and humanity will be saved, but the group I belong to, the Dulcinium Utilitarian Creed movement, is I now realise, a little fanatical. My friend Victor is harmless. He is just as misguided as I was. His chemist colleague Ramon is firmly committed and will be a hard one to convince that his work is wrong. The two chemists, Victor and Ramon are working on the antidote in an apartment on Calle de Granollers. When this is complete they will release the virus TX25C into the city water supply. There are two quantitites of this virus and they are kept in the Banco De Espana on Placa Catalunya

Steve Kenning

and Caixa Catalunya on Calle de Provenca in bank security deposit boxes. There is no doubt that you can put a stop to this madness. I can't. I know that the others suspect me of trying to end all their work. Brother Xavi is a politician who is totally committed to the Millenarium ideals of his mentor Alberto Carboner. It is his vision we are following. He is a strong man, not evil but willing to do anything to achieve his lifelong ambition of enabling the rebirth of the Millenarium. However, it is his lifelong colleague, ally and henchman whom I fear most of all, Father Jordi. He is completely devoid of any kind of logic or humanity, despite his ordination as a priest. He has a belief and that is all. He will do whatever it takes to achieve it and his message always comes from Brother Xavi. I fear that I am his next victim. I have wronged the creed and I am a risk to its success. This is the reason why I am sending you this letter. I do warn you Albert, be very careful. Even your detective friend Ferran cannot save you from this madman, Jordi. He works outside the normal boundaries and he seems to move in a different dimension. Please act on my words but beware.

Thank you for listening and good luck.

Your brother in law,

Jorge.

Reason to Believe

This letter as Albert read it felt damp. It had been sealed in an envelope hat had probably been on the floor of his apartment for up to a day, a day in which the weather had been poor, rain and more rain. Albert thought about this but it didn't fully explain the feeling of humidity the paper held. Albert looked at the writing again and re-read the letter. He was alone now in his apartment and he felt a chill. The letter unnerved him. He already knew most of its contents but it also carried a warning of an unseen threat. He walked along the long apartment corridor with the letter in his hand and reached out for the telephone on the mantelpiece above the mock English fireplace in the living room. The phone rang several times.

'Ferran, where are you?' Albert shouted out in frustration.

Then the phone clicked off the hook.

'Hello? Who is it?'

'Ferran? This is Albert. Albert Roig.'

'Ahh. I was just thinking of you Albert. What news do you have?'

'I have a letter Ferran. It is a letter from Jorge. It gives us the information we need. But it also...'

At that point Albert was grabbed forcibly around the neck. He didn't see the hands coming and he didn't see where they came from. He fell to the ground heavily with the two strong hands firmly clasped around his neck. He couldn't breathe. The hands were strangling him, preventing even an ounce of air from reaching his lungs. His head hit the hard tiled floor, stunning him. The phone clattered across the floor.

'Albert! Albert! What is happening? Albert!' shouted Ferran at the phone as he was aware of some kind of disturbance.

A cloaked hand picked up the phone and placed it carefully on the small brown wood coffee table. Slowly and with purpose he moved the few steps towards Albert's prostrate body. He placed one leg on the tiled floor between Albert's arm and his waist, then, he deliberately put his other foot in the parallel position on the fallen man's other side. To do this he had to move Albert's arm slightly away from its resting place next to his body. The large frame of the cloaked priest stood astride his victim. He smiled. Albert lay beneath him, spreadeagled on the floor, in some kind of prosaic shape.

'Albert Roig, you need to have no worries about the fate of this world no more.'

As he spoke he spread out his hands and reached down once again for the bruised neck of his helpless victim. He looked at Albert's prone body. Then he closed his eyes and faced towards heaven and gripped the neck.

'Servo is letalis animus.'

Reason to Believe

Divine intervention was unexpected, but it came at that very moment. Out of nowhere flew a heavy metal cooking pot. It was attached to the arms of a woman. Before he had chance to open his eyes the pot hit the man's head with real momentum.

The arms belonged to Montse. She had returned home at the exact moment her husband was attacked by the cloaked priest. As she entered their apartment silently, moving into the living room she immediately witnessed the aftermath of the attack on her husband. Restraining her natural emotion and the desire to take instant action, she had quickly entered the kitchen from the hallway and picked up a huge steel frying pan. Before the priest could harm her husband further she swung the pan against his head. The impact of the frying pan on his head sent him sprawling wildly across the floor. He released Albert's neck from his grip and was flailing around helplessly with his arms, shocked by the unexpected interruption to his work. She looked at the priest, as he lay crumpled on the floor. Should she hit him again? Should she help her husband? Should she phone the police? As she considered her next move she lost the opportunity to strike the priest again. As she looked back towards him from visually assessing the condition of her husband, she realised that he had gone. Then the door to the apartment slammed shut. She had no interest in going after the injured priest. Instead, she noticed the phone placed on the table and faintly heard a voice calling from it. She picked it up. Ferran was still there. He had heard everything.

'Who is that?' he demanded.

'Montse, it's Montse, Albert is hurt.'

'Don't worry,' said Ferran, 'Help is on its way. What does he look like? The attacker?'

'He's a priest, a fuckin priest,' screamed Montse into the phone. She threw the phone down and ran over to Albert who was unconscious on the floor. She saw the bruises on his neck. She was relieved that he appeared to be breathing, although with difficulty. Instinctively she felt for his pulse. It was there. He was still alive. Quickly she rushed to the kitchen and grabbed a glass of water. Kneeling next to her husband on the wooden floor she forced the water down his throat as she cradled his head in her hands.

Within minutes Montse was sitting next to her husband in an ambulance heading for the hospital. The paramedics said he would be alright. Montse, relieved, was determined to be strong for him whatever. She held his hand in an iron grip.

Reason to Believe

33

Initially it appeared that the clues left behind at the crime scene were once again minimal. The large apartment living room, fed by a long narrow corridor leading to the entrance door, revealed evidence nothing more obvious than a few fibres and, once again, those large size eleven sandal prints. This time however, his team had also found saliva traces on the floor where Albert's assailant had landed after being felled by Montse's pan. Ferran stood still in the living room looking at the crime scene hand on hip, with the other hand holding back his long, lank, black hair. He looked puzzled, although he was in a state of complete concentration.

'Will! Will!'

Steve Kenning

The voice of Ferran's long-time lover and detective partner, Maria, rang through the silence.

'Will, we've got Xavi.'

Ferran looked at his partner as she raced towards him excitedly along the apartment entrance corridor. She stopped and beckoned him to follow her. Slowly he internalised and assimilated her words. Then he simply nodded and automatically followed her out of the apartment. Within minutes they were at the Mossos d'Esquadra headquarters on Gran Via. They left Maria's white Seat on the pavement outside the grand old converted four storey building in the heart of the Eixample. The evening was balmly as they strolled purposefully towards the entrance to the historical building.

Inside the two detectives quickly passed through the brightly lit entrance hall and headed for one of the cell floors that lay below ground level. The old building that was the home to the Mossos in this part of Barcelona was ridiculously grand inside. It looked nothing like a police station should. Several ornately crafted apartments had been knocked together to create a police station full of small rooms and unusually designed meeting places. The circular stairwell that the two detectives were racing down was wide and high, with grey marble steps, magnolia walls and light provided by huge glass chandeliers, relics from the buildings previous life. At the bottom of the stairs and along a narrow

Reason to Believe

corridor Ferran and Maria eventually came to a white door. They knocked and waited. Almost immediately the white door opened and they were greeted by a female police officer. They entered the stunningly bright, white room. There was nothing in the room except a grey plastic table with metal legs and a white patio chair. Everything else was white, the floor, the walls and the ceiling.

Sitting at the table on the only chair in the room was an elderly man, probably in his sixties, smartly dressed and prominently displaying a well-coiffured goaty beard. He sat upright and proud in his chair and tried to look comfortable in the bleak surroundings. He stared at his visitors.

'At last, someone of seniority I believe. I have been speaking to this women for over an hour now and she will not reply to my questions,' he said nodding towards the policewoman.

'Perhaps you can tell me who you are and why I am here.'

All the time he stared at Ferran. Maria took exception to being ignored. She immediately summed this character up as an arrogant chauvinist.

'I am Detective Maria Fernandez Tupelo and this is Detective Will Ferran,' she answered pointing to her tall, dark haired colleague. Ferran let her get on with it and walked over to the wall before casually leaning against it.

Steve Kenning

The man was a little taken aback by Maria's forcefulness and tried to maintain eye contact with Ferran but Ferran was having none of it, he just stared at Maria. She continued,

'Xavier Bosch you are here under suspicion of terrorist offences and also to help us with our investigations relating to a couple of current cases, one of murder and the other of attempted murder. We have reason to believe you may be either involved with both these cases or at the very least acquainted with the people involved.'

Xavi leant back in his chair aghast.

'I beg your pardon? Do you know who I am?'

'Xavier Bosch,' repeated Maria in a monosyllabic tone.

'I am an Episcopus Vagan, an envoy to his holiness Pope Benedict XVI.,' he stated with importance.

'To me you are simply Xavier Bosch,' repeated Maria.

The older man was clearly intensely annoyed by this impudent woman. It was written all over his face.

'I have diplomatic immunity and the freedom of your city. How dare you incarcerate me here in this dreadful place full of sinners. How can you believe that someone of my faith could be involved in any wrongdoing? How can you treat me with such contempt?' The grey haired man stuttered with indignation.

'Mr Bosch, what do you know about a movement called the Utilitarian Dulcinian Creed?' asked a calm, determined

Reason to Believe

Maria clearly relishing the control she had over this arrogant man.

'This is ridiculous,' flustered Xavi Bosch. He stood up in frustration and started to walk away from his chair.

'Sit down!' boomed Ferran from the side of the room. Xavi stopped immediately and looked towards the source of the voice.

'Do as he says,' echoed Maria.

Without a word Xavi sat down, obviously a little deflated.

'Now answer my question,' pursued Maria.

'Who? What? I don't know what you are talking about. In my role I meet many people. I need my lawyer, I will not answer any of your questions until he is here.'

Xavi folded his arms and looked straight ahead.

Maria glanced over to Ferran. The huge detective, all six foot five of him, reached into his jacket pocket and pulled out an A4 brown envelope. He carefully opened it up and drew out a colour photograph. Without saying a word he walked over to the grey table and placed the photograph in front of the mute Xavi. The older man refused to look at it.

'An interesting picture,' interrupted Maria, 'Notice the time and date in the corner. The picture was taken outside the apartment of Senor Tomeu Moncada several minutes after he was killed. The picture is definitely you and it appears that you have an accomplice, a priest, it looks like a certain Father Jordi Pique. We have many more images from CCTV cameras and from satellite cameras. There are several more pictures of you in this location at this particular time and others of you with members of the Utilitarian Dulcinian Creed. We have plenty to implicate you. You think you are very clever and you are very careful to leave no traces behind after your evil actions, but you are not generation Y are you, you didn't even consider the power of modern technology, did you?' mocked Maria.

Xavi, bothered by Maria's words, glanced at the photograph. His face was slowly turning grey with fear. Ferran had been watching the grey haired man closely. He moved towards him.

'I suggest you tell us everything you know. Your dream of creating a new Millenarium is over. We will soon find your chemical store and we will pick up your remaining associates, all three of them.'

Xavi looked surprised both by Ferran's intervention and his words. He composed himself slightly before responding.

'You are wrong. I will succeed in my aims but I repeat that I do not know what you are talking about,' he replied cryptically and with a sense of menace.

'This is your last chance before we put you in a cell for twenty-four hours. A man of your grooming would find that difficult to manage,' rasped Maria.

'You are an evil man Detective Ferran and so you will not be spared,' stated Xavi ignoring Maria once again, 'Your

Reason to Believe

time will come and soon I am sure. I am not scared, I have the Lord on my side,' continued a smug Xavi.

Maria and Ferran exchanged glances and shrugged simultaneously.

'Take him away!' instructed Maria to the female guard.

As Xavi was led reluctantly out of the room Maria whispered to Ferran, 'What exactly is an Episcopus Vagan? Anything to do with meat?' she smiled. Ferran chuckled quietly before enlightening her.

'I've come across one once before, in the Pyrenees. They are a little weird, they are something out of another long-gone age.'

'What are they then?' Maria asked.

'They are people who have been consecrated as Bishops outside the usual law of the Church. They have no generally recognized diocese. I think the term is Latin and means "wandering bishops".' Replied Ferran smiling at the thought that they had caught an Episcopus Vagan.

34

'Are you sure that is the alarm from Brother Xavi?' asked a nervous Victor.

Ramon looked at his colleague in exasperation.

'You know it is. If anyone is taken by the police or is in personal danger, they set off the alarm with their mobile phone, and if the green pager goes off then it is Brother Xavi. You know that.'

Victor was nervous and unsure. He was tall and overweight with his black hair and full black beard making him appear larger than he actually was. He dwarfed the sharp-suited, clean cut Ramon.

The two men were exhausted and tired of each other after spending the past week working and living together in

Reason to Believe

a small apartment on the outskirts of the city developing an antidote to the virus. They were still a long way from success.

'We must release the virus. That was the instruction if Xavi was taken,' announced Ramon.

'No! We don't know he has been taken. It has been less than a day since we last saw him,' reacted Victor unusually strongly.

'It is our purpose Victor. We have given our word. You know it is our destiny. Do not be afraid, we are doing our Lord's work.'

Victor gave Ramon an unconvinced look.

'Not yet, we cannot release the virus until the antidote is ready,' reacted Victor.

'We must. You stay here and continue to work on the antidote. I will go to the virus store and prepare for its release into the water supply of the city,' added Ramon.

Victor looked horrified as Ramon unhitched his jacket from the coat hook on the back of the door. He put it on and walked towards the door that led out of the apartment. The gentle, bearded Victor looked around in panic, searching for an answer. His eyes fixed on a wooden mallet. He grabbed it and raced after Ramon. Ramon was opening the outside door to the apartment as Victor flew at him. In one violent move the huge bearded man swung the mallet and fiercely struck his colleague full on the top of his head. Ramon

233

collapsed instantly and fell in a crumpled heap onto the floor. The bearded giant of a man didn't even look down at Ramon. Instead he rushed out of the door into the outside hallway and leapt down the stairs of the internal fire escape.

Reason to Believe

35

By the time Ferran reached the hospital, several hours had passed since Albert Roig had been attacked. Nobody from the family had been in contact with him so he had no idea of Albert's condition, he hoped for the best. Ferran felt quite confident that he wasn't going to get an unpleasant surprise, as he was sure that someone would have told him if Albert had died from his wounds. Inside the hospital the tall, lean detective ate up the steps two at a time as he raced up to the fourth floor. Within minutes he was on the top floor of the modern building. He was fit, but not as fit as he would like to be. He gasped a little as he walked along the gleamimg hospital corridor looking for Albert.

Steve Kenning

'Can I help you?' enquired a middle age nurse, short with brown hair tinted with the occasional blonde streak.

'Yes, thank you. Albert Roig?'

'Ah, yes, you would be?' she enquired with impressive caution.

'Detective Ferran of the Mossos,' replied Ferran routinely displaying his badge encased in its leather wallet to the nurse.

'OK, follow me.'

The slim nurse moved with some speed and Ferran had to walk quicker than his natural lugubrious stride in order to keep pace with her. The two of them passed along several corridors and through a couple of wards until they came to a private room at the back of the hospital. A policeman was sitting attentively on a chair in the corridor just outside Albert's room. The nurse knocked on the wooden door, waited a second then put her head around it and said something. Then she stood back and signalled Ferran to go into the room.

'Hello, Will,' said a sprightly, bright eyed Albert, who was sitting up in his bed. He had a huge bandage around his head and a mixture of white gauze and plasters on one side of his neck.

Ferran was a little surprised by Alberts condition, but then immediately showed his delight. He smiled broadly and walked over to hug Albert. Montse was also in the room

Reason to Believe

sitting on a chair on the opposite side of the bed, she stood up and hugged Ferran as he moved around the bed towards her. Ferran felt her relief.

'You look great apart from the turban. How are you?' asked the Detective.

'I feel really good but I woke up about two hours ago with a terrible headache. Apparently when I fell, I crashed my head on the hard stone tiles. They gave me some tablets and now I feel fine,' chirped Albert.

'What about your neck?' questioned the detective surprised by the lucidity shown by Albert.

'He was very lucky,' sighed a relieved Montse, 'Nothing is broken but he has a bruised windpipe and severe lacerations on his neck.'

'So did you catch the guy that did this? The priest?' asked Albert with a hopeful edge to his voice.

'Unfortunately not, but we are closing in on them. We have picked up the leader of the Creed, Xavier Bosch,' replied Ferran.

Albert and Montse looked disappointed and a little worried by this news. Ferran sensed their concern.

'Listen, you are safe, you have a guard and there is only one man likely to come after you and he doesn't have the element of surprise any more. You need to rest tonight and tomorrow we can discuss how to solve this problem without putting you into any more danger,' said Ferran.

Steve Kenning

'What do you mean? I need to find the grave of Fra Dolcino. We have found out that there has been a great amount of deception and illusion, but I do not want to risk failing to carry out the requests of Senor Moncada,' retorted an aggravated Albert.

'But you know that your father in law misled you about the orb you saw, surely you can see that he has probably misled you about everything else,' countered an exasperated Ferran.

'No, I don't agree with you Ferran,' responded Albert, 'I think he drew me into the illusion to make sure I carried out his wishes. He wanted, needed me, to believe what he was telling me. Anyhow, we know that Vittoria's husband, Jorge, was working on a chemical designed to poison the people of this city. This coupled with the fact that someone tried to kill me today makes me believe we have to stop this Millenarium.'

Albert was red in the face with exertion. Montse stood over him and placed her hand on his head calmingly.

'Albert, we will get to the grave, but not today. You need to sleep,' she said comfortingly.

Ferran walked backwards and forwards around the bed frustrated.

'You will, I know, do what you feel you have to do. But, if you go on this adventure to the Pyrenees I really cannot

Reason to Believe

guarantee your safety. Please stay in the city,' pleaded the Detective.

Albert stared back at him with a determined look on his face that told Ferran exactly the opposite to what he wanted to hear. The initial friendliness of their meeting had disappeared, replaced by a sense of dissatisfaction as all three of them shared opposing viewpoints. Ferran sensed that there was no way he was going to win this one and decided it was time to go.

'Ok, keep me informed Albert. If you need help let me know and I will see what I can do. Promise me that you will keep me informed of your movements,' requested the Detective.

'We will,' smiled Albert in return.

Ferran shook Albert's hand and hugged Montse before leaving the small private ward.

Outside the private room, in the hospital corridor, Ferran pressed a couple of buttons on his mobile.

'Maria, where are you?' he asked, before waiting for a reply. He didn't have to wait long. He listened carefully.

'Ok, I'll see you in Bar Colombo in fifteen minutes. We need to find this laboratory and the crazy priest. We have only about twelve hours before Albert heads to the Pyrenees,' concluded Ferran.

36

With the inner satisfaction that Albert was recovering safely in hospital with Montse by his side, Florita and Christy left the hospital at midday having decided to continue the research the four of them had started the day before.

They sat around a circular glass table in Florita's modern apartment a couple of streets away from Calle Balmes in the Padua area of the city. The table was in the centre of a kitchen/diner with floor to ceiling windows that opened out onto a large balcony. At this moment neither sister had any time for taking in the panoramic view across the city from the tall windows, they were engrossed and pre-occupied by the task ahead of them. The attack on Albert had made them

Reason to Believe

all realise that they were not just involved in an adventurous game. They now knew that they were actually involved in something that was deadly serious. As a result, they were both vividly aware that it was imperative for them to find the exact location of Fra Dolcino's grave, and also to confirm the exact words that Albert would have to say in order to end this Millennium madness.

'Remember the words we found a few days ago at the University library Florita?' said Christy.

'Yes, we wrote them down somewhere,' replied her sister.

'I know, I have them here. I thought they were the words that would stop this Millenarium movement, but now I'm not so sure,' continued Christy with a concerned expression on her face.   She shuffled through a couple of folders of paper, and eventually after several minutes, she pulled out of a purple folder, an A4 sheet of paper with her scrawly writing all over it.

'Here it is,' she stated before reading the words on the sheet,

'Thou who perchance,
shalt shortly view the sun, this warning thou,
bear to Dolcino – bid him, if he wish not
here soon to follow me, that with good store,
of food he arm him, lest imprisoning snows
yield him a victim to Novara'a power

no easy conquest else.'

There was a pause as she finished reading.

'Well it sounds impressive to me,' commented Florita, 'But I don't understand what it means. To be honest I think I agree with you, I can't really see how it relates to releasing Fra Dolcino or empowering the Millenarium.'

Christy let out a huge sigh.

'Well Florita, I do have a real problem with this the more I think about. I can't see the relevance. Why read out these words? This isn't magic, its reality. Words can't stop all this. I wonder if Alfonso Carboner was actually just extremely clever and foresaw every possibility. This could be just a trail he has laid for anyone who might one day try to stop his work,' responded Christy.

Florita nodded in slow agreement whilst she considered her sisters theory.

'That would explain why only some of his diary was published on the internet. Yet it wasn't hard to find the words needed to stop the Millenarium now was it?' added Florita.

'Exactly! My thoughts too sister, so I looked at the thing that Alfonso Carboner was obsessed with. In all his writing he comes back to it time and time again,' continued Christy.

'What was that?' questioned her sister.

'The Divine Comedy, that great poem by Dante.'

Reason to Believe

Florita waited, mouth open, expectantly for an explanation.

'It seems to me that Alfonso Carboner was obsessed by this poem and if you notice he refers to it at least eighty times in his diary. I thought it was a good bet to look into it further,' Christy revealed with a sarcastic edge to her voice.

'So tell me what did you find? I can tell you are excited by something, remember, I know you well,' stated Florita.

Christy settled back into her seat and with outstretched arms opened her pink A4 folder. There on the first page was her evidence. She opened the folder clips and removed the first piece of paper in the folder and handed it to Florita.

Florita read it to herself then looked up at Christy in excitement.

'Yes Christy, you have it. I didn't realise before. But I do remember it now, we read it at school and that particular point was always highlighted. How did you spot that?'

'It was easy,' replied Christy, 'I looked on Wikipedia and it told me. It told me that the last word in each of the three parts of the Divine Comedy is "stars".'

'So, what does that mean?' asked Florita.

'Well,' added Christy, 'The Inferno is an account of Dante's own journey, guided by the ancient Roman poet Virgil, through the nine levels of hell. During this journey Dante encounters and holds conversations with the souls of the damned. At the end of the journey, at the bottom of hell,

Steve Kenning

Dante must face Satan and confront the problem of how to escape from the underworld.'

'Fascinating,' said a sarcastic Florita, 'But what exactly does that mean?'

'Well sister, I think it is simple. Dante was trying to escape hell basically, and the way to do that was to think of stars and the heavenly association of them. So, I think all Albert needs to say at the grave of Fra Dolcino is 'stars'.'

Christy stopped and thought for a little while. As she did so Florita observed her closely and in doing so sensed a slight disturbance in her sister.

'What is it Christy? What it is that concerns you? I thought you were sure about this?'

Christy looked up at her elder sister and smiled.

'I think that the answer to this riddle is actually quite simple. We have to do nothing. We simply have to believe in what we believe in. We have to have a reason to believe. I am sure that Dante's 'stars' was all about people believing in themselves, people having a reason to believe. He defeated Satan by believing in himself. So, we need to do nothing other than believe in ourselves and to do what we have to do.'

Florita stared at her sister and thought for some time about what she had said. After several minutes she replied.

'So what do we actually do?'

Reason to Believe

37

'I need to satisfy my Lord.'

'I need to satisfy my Lord.'

'I need to satisfy my Lord.'

A huge hulk of a figure, clad in black, was rocking from side to side, chanting the same words over and over again.

'Please Lord direct me, what do I need to do? I need your guidance.'

'I need your guidance,' he repeated.

'I need your guidance my Lord.'

The huge man was standing with his forehead pressed against the stone wall above the main doorway into the monastery at Pedralbes in the east of the city. People were watching him but making very sure that they walked well away from him. No one dared to approach this massive, captivated priest.

Twenty minutes later he was alone. His head was bloodied from its pounding on the arched rock doorway that formed the main entrance to the monastery. Without reason after twenty minutes or so of self-flagellation, he stood away from the building and stopped the self-harming.

He turned away from the wall and sprayed his arms up towards the stars.

'Tell me my Lord. What is it that I need to do to satisfy your needs, I am your servant?'

These words were shouted out and then in a state of complete exhaustion he slumped to his knees.

As he lay there in a state of suspended animation, exhausted by his vigil, in his head he heard some words. He was sure it was his Lord. He had heard the voice before, although not as distantly. He stopped rocking and concentrated hard in order to hear exactly what was being said. His head was bleeding, and mingled with the sweat from his exertion, a scarlet stream ran down his face and onto his dog collar. He listened.

'Help me! Help me! I need you to help me.'

'I will my Lord, I will. Tell me how,' replied the bloodied priest.

'You are the only true believer, you are my one true disciple,' he heard a voice say in his head.

Reason to Believe

'Thank you my Lord, I am you servant. What do you need me to do for you? You know I am your servant.'

He was kneeling on the stone steps that led up the side of the monastery. He was alone, nobody was coming anywhere near him. His location, where he was kneeling, was usually a thoroughfare but anyone who started down or up the steps saw him immediately and changed their route. This large bloodied priest was talking to himself with a crazed look in his eyes. No one was likely to risk a confrontation. A small crowd of people collected at the bottom of the steps watching him. A couple were on their mobile phones contacting the police. Jordi sensed something was wrong.

'My Lord, I must go,' he stated, looking furtively around.

'Yes, my disciple you must go and do the Lords work. The mission is almost complete. The plague is almost upon us. It will rid the world of evil. Do what you must do to foil Satan,' were the words of comfort that resonated in his head.

Jordi wiped his eyes on his sleeves and then raised himself from the ground. He stood upright with his headthrown back. He looked dreadful and horrific. This sudden movement scattered the little crowd of onlookers. He heard a siren. He moved up the steps along the side of the monastery and strode through an archway and out towards the openness of the Colserolla Hills.

38

'Are you sure you are alright Albert?' asked a concerned Montse as her husband took a seat on their sofa back in their apartment in the suburbs of the city. He had just arrived home after being released from hospital. He looked fine but she sensed he wasn't. He seemed pre-occupied.

'I am fine. I just can't stop thinking about the future and what we need to do,' he replied.

Montse sat down next to her husband.

'What do you mean? Are you worried about being strong enough to make the journey to the Pyrenees?'

Albert said nothing for a moment.

Reason to Believe

'No,' he started, 'I am just wondering why I should go to the grave of Fra Dolcino.'

'You must Albert, I will help you,' replied a worried Montse.

'I know you will support me Montse, I know you are a wonderful wife. But, I just wonder if it is necessary.'

Montse looked seriously concerned.

'It was what Papa asked you to do.'

'Exactly!' replied Albert.

'Do you think Papa was lying?'

Albert looked her in the eyes.

'I think he has always lied to us. He was not the person we thought he was. He lied to me about the orb and I think he has lied to us about what we need to do. Ferran is right. For some reason he wants us out of the city. I felt it might be so they can release the virus. If we are all out of the city then you are all safe.'

'But Vittoria and Adrianna would still be here,' questioned Montse.

'You know as well as I do that Papa is besotted with you and Florita. He would have stopped at you two, it was only your mother that wanted more children.'

Montse reflected on her husband's words. Then she had a further thought.

'You have been thinking about this for a while haven't you, tell me all you are thinking.'

Steve Kenning

Montse sat next to Albert and pinned him with her eyes. Albert said nothing at first, but he knew he would eventually have to say something.

'Montse are you sure you want me to tell you all my thoughts? They do not put Papa in a good light and I may be wrong.'

'Albert, I love you and I trust you. I have never known you to be wrong. Papa I love too, but I know he has many faults. Please tell me your thoughts. Please tell me from the beginning,' replied Montse, holding onto to her husbands arm tenderly as she spoke.

Albert paused and chose his words carefully.

'Ok. I had doubts at first when I first met your father in the Ciutat Vella. I sensed that he had another agenda. He has always liked me, but he would never consider me to be someone who would lie. Remember when we had that argument about the politics of the country when we first got together? I argued with him just to impress you, to show you that I was a strong man with my own views. Then I lied and he knew it. That's partly why he got so annoyed with me,' began Albert. He saw the concerned look of his wife in his eyes.

'Let's have a drink, it will make this easier.'

He started to get up from the sofa. Montse sensed that he was struggling and put her hand across him to keep him sitting.

Reason to Believe

'Albert. I'll go. She jumped up and rushed into the kitchen. A couple of minutes later she returned with two glasses and a bottle of red wine. She placed the glasses on the small dark brown table in front of them and poured the wine into them.

'So Albert,' she said handing him a glass of wine, 'Tell me.'

Albert sipped his wine and gulped silently. Eventually he started to reveal his thoughts.

'I didn't realise it until I was attacked. I saw that my attacker was a priest and I wondered, as he was attacking me, how he knew me, how he knew where I lived, and exactly how he had an intimate knowledge of the layout of the apartment. You just wouldn't know where to go in our apartment if you were a stranger as there are so many doors from the main hallway. As I lay bleeding and unconscious my brain must have started quietly sifting information because as soon as I came round in the hospital I had a great many questions. I looked back at the things your father told me and I questioned them, I also remembered reading the Diary of Alfonso Carboner. Throughout it there was a mention of getting confirmation from 'Mon'. This was undoubtedly his lover. Alfonso Carboner was unashamedly and openly gay, this was revealed in the Montserrat chronicles that explained the reason for him being asked to leave the monastery.'

Steve Kenning

'Are you saying that my father was 'Mon' his lover?' Asked a shocked Montse. She let go of Albert and sat back against the sofa. Albert reached out for her and held her arm.

'I am convinced. If we want to find out the exact truth, I would think our friend Detective Ferran could easily investigate further and find old colleagues who would confirm it,' countered Albert.

They both remained silent for a while.

'Go on,' Montse said eventually.

Albert paused before laying his thoughts out in front of his wife, 'I don't think your father is dead.'

'What?' shrieked Montse.

Albert picked up one of the old books off the coffee table and flicked through the pages looking for a particular section.

'Here is a chapter in the illusion book about 'faking' death. All you need to do is to administer a particular drug. Apparently it puts your body to sleep for twenty-four hours and makes the heart rate unreadable.'

As he spoke he sensed Montse's disbelief.

'Let's go and look at the body in the mortuary. I bet it has disappeared.'

Reason to Believe

39

Ramon was sitting on the tiled floor of the apartment gently rubbing his head. It really hurt and he was having trouble focussing on his watch face. Eventually his sight cleared a little and he saw it was a couple hours later than the last time he had looked. He was still dazed, a little giddy and disorientated when he eventually got to his feet. As the blood started to circulate more quickly around his body he suddenly remembered what had happened.

'It was Victor, Victor did this to me.'

Quickly he looked around the room for his jacket. He saw it resting across the back of the sofa and hurried over to it. He picked up the plain black jacket and rustled through the inside pockets. He found a pager and punched in a message before sending it. Then with his jacket over his arm he made an unsteady move for the hallway. He tottered along clumsily and headed out of the apartment into the outside lobby. Within a few minutes he was three floors down, and out onto the quiet suburban street.

Something stirred in his smock pocket. Jordi reached inside and pulled out a small black plastic pager. It was flashing red and making a shrill high-pitched noise. He looked at the brief message that ran across the LED screen.

'Victor has gone.'

Father Jordi knew exactly what the message meant and what he had to do. He was tired and hungry but he had been through harder situations. His life was not about pleasure or self-satisfaction, it was about service to his Lord. Over the past hour or so he had moved steadily across the Colserolla Hills that edged the city. He had been heading towards Tibidabo to clear his head and be closer to his Lord by standing outside the church of Sagrat Cor, set at the highest point in the city. Following the message on his pager, without really thinking, he changed direction and headed across several hills. Eventually he found himself just outside a metro station that led directly down into the Padua district. His immediate task was to find Victor.

Reason to Believe

40

'Has he said anything yet?' asked Ferran.

'Nothing. He looks shattered but I can see he is smiling inside at us. He knows that we know what he is involved in, even though he is admitting nothing, but he also knows that we know too little. He knows we can do nothing,' replied a frustrated Maria. Her sultry dark looks appearing as if they were about to explode.

Ferran frowned and paced around the office of the Special Investigations Unit (SIU) that was situated on the third floor of a converted building on Via Laeitana.

'What do you make of this?'

Ferran changed tack and handed the black pager over to Maria.

Steve Kenning

'What is it?'

'Xavi's pager. Look at the message.'

The pager LED screen said, 'Victor has gone'.

Maria looked up at Ferran.

'Who is Victor? Is he one of the Creed?' she asked.

'He must be. But what does it mean? Has Victor left them, has he gone to release the virus? What?'

Maria went pale in the face as she suddenly remembered something from earlier in the day.

'On no!'

'What?' reacted a worried Ferran as he moved towards Maria.

Maria looked at her boss and her lover in the eyes and reached out to hold his arm. Her eyes were looking for forgiveness.

'A couple of hours ago there was a message left on my mobile from a small Mossos office in Padua saying that a man had walked in claiming that he had a virus that he was about to release into the city water supply. The officer who left the message was laughing as he thought it was a joke. The guy was large and wild looking. The officer didn't believe him. I just didn't put two and two together. It's so obvious,' Maria revealed distraughtly.

'Don't worry, where is this guy now?' said a purposeful Ferran.

Reason to Believe

'I presume he's in the cells at the office,' replied Maria, 'I'll give them a call.'

Instantly she returned a call to the number left on her mobile.

Steve Kenning

41

'We're here to see this big guy you have in your cells, Victor Jose Gimenez. Can we see him?' demanded Ferran purposefully as he and Maria strode into the small foyer of the Mossos d'Esquadra station located on a backstreet in Padua in the rich suburbs of the city.

'Who are you?' responded the bored young clean-cut officer sitting behind the desk in the foyer. His mistake was to stay leaning back lazily in his seat showing a distinct lack of respect for his visitors. Without replying Ferran reached across the small counter, grabbed the collar of the young officer and pressed his face onto the ceramic counter before slamming his black leather i.d down right under the nose of the dull eyed young officer. Ferran released him and the

Reason to Believe

shocked young officer jumped into action. With one swift movement the young man stood up and led Ferran and Maria out of the lobby into a small corridor. Suddenly, there was purpose in the face of the officer.

'He is just along here. There is no one else in our cells,' he said as he walked. He was trying to be as helpful and knowledgeable as he could possibly be.

'We only have four cells.'

'How long has he been here?' asked Ferran.

'Two, maybe three hours,' replied the nervous young officer.

'Has anyone taken a statement from him,' questioned Maria.

'I think so. If they have it will be in the front office. I will look for you in a moment. I have only been on duty for the last hour,' Then remembering more useful information he continued, 'Oh, I did let a priest in to see him about half an hour ago.'

'A priest?' responded a concerned Maria.

'Yes, he said that the Church were visiting all temporary occupants of police cells, as most were drunks, to try to persuade them to lead a 'better life',' smiled the young officer as they passed through another door.

'Here we are.'

Steve Kenning

He placed a key into the lock of the first door they came to. He turned it and pushed the door open, standing back to let the two detectives into the cell.

'Oh no!' sighed Ferran in despair as he entered the cell. Maria, who was close behind him, simply put her hand to her mouth instinctively.

'What?' said the young officer following the two detectives into the small cell.

The three of them stood still looking down at the huge hulk of Victor. He was sitting on a bench, leaning against the cell wall. He looked as if he was asleep, although they all knew he wasn't, as his head was at a right angle to his body. His neck had been broken and his body was lifeless.

Ferran was livid.

'I want a full statement, description and CCTV footage within ten minutes. And I want your name and rank. Also, find me the report from earlier,' he barked.

The young officer was shaking with fear and embarrassment but managed to pull himself together to rush back to the main office to find the report.

'Get our team down here Maria. We need to get what we can from this mess.'

'I'm sorry Ferran. I should have reacted earlier when I got the call. It's not the young guys fault,' apologised Maria.

'No excuse,' he stated firmly, 'A prisoner should be safe in a cell. No excuse,' he repeated and walked out along the

Reason to Believe

corridor. He ran into the young officer half way along the long corridor that led back to the main entrance foyer. In his hand the young man had a few papers.

'Detective Ferran, I have the report here,' he said as he thrust the papers towards the tall dark haired detective.

Ferran quickly read the brief report. He looked at the young officer, 'Expect a team of detectives from the SIU within minutes. Give them all the help you can.'

'Yes sir, I will,' replied the nervous officer.

'Maria, look at this,' said Ferran handing her the report, 'We need to move quickly.'

Maria read the report as she walked following Ferran out of the building.

42

'So you are saying that Papa was lying to us and probably has been for all our lives?' questioned an angry Florita.

Christy was just sitting on the wooden kitchen chair with her mouth open staring at her sister Montse.

'It makes sense. Think about it. Everything points to what I am saying being true,' replied the elder sister.

'Pah!' retorted Florita indignantly.

The three sisters sat around the kitchen table deflated and silent. They sat there for quite a time quietly fuming with each other before Albert considered it safe to speak.

'It will not do us any good to argue about this,' he said calmly, 'We can only surmise about your father and it will do us no good to dwell on it any more at this moment in

Reason to Believe

time. We have to take far more important action and we need to move forward. It is interesting that for whatever reason we have all come to the same conclusion about our next course of action, that we have no need to go to the grave of Fra Dulcino. I think we are agreed that we must stay in the city?' Albert asked.

Florita was still looking at her sister with disbelief in her eyes. She glanced across the table towards Albert and paused before speaking.

'We agree Albert. We stay in the city and find the people behind the Dulcinian Creed. The need for this 'perfect person' to go the grave of Fra Dolcino to recite some words to stop Armageddon always did seem a little far fetched to me,' said Florita in a reasonably calm and conciliatory voice.

Christy had tears in her eyes and had been sitting quietly listening.

'I think you may be right about Papa,' she said quietly returning to the topic Albert was keen to move away from. The other three looked at her expectantly waiting for her words. Again she spoke quietly.

'I woke up mid afternoon in Mama and Papa's apartment several years ago. You know when I was having problems with drugs. I had nowhere else to go and Mama was really supportive and trying her best to get me through a really bad time. Anyway I was stoned most the time then and what I heard on that afternoon didn't register until now. Many of the things that happened during that time keep flashing back into my mind as if it was yesterday. It is only just a few minutes ago, after you said what you said about Papa Albert, that I have ever remembered this.'

The other three were captivated by this revelation.

'What did you remember?' asked Albert.

'Well, Mama and Papa were arguing about something. I was about to walk out of my bedroom but the door was ajar and I heard them, so I stopped and listened. They were arguing, but not loudly. She was really cross with him, something she never revealed in front of us, the children.'

The sharing of this new memory was building tension in her two sisters. Florita couldn't take it anymore, she blurted out, 'What happened Christy? You are taking an age to tell us.'

Christy half smiled then solemnly continued.

'You must accept that what I am to tell you may not be true,' she said with a concerned look on her face, 'I loved Mama and I truly love Papa, but at that time I was so into the drugs that nothing seemed real,' she paused again.

'I remember this now as if it was yesterday. Mama said to Papa 'I have supported you like a wife for a long time and borne you five daughters, with your manhood revered by many, as you insisted. I have allowed you to lead a double life, whilst I have sacrificed a life without a man's touch and his physical love. I love you and always will, but I will not

Reason to Believe

tolerate you bringing remnants of your 'other' life into my house.' Then she obviously held something up as there was a pause and a slight noise.'

'What was it?' asked a captivated Montse, 'What did she hold up?'

'Well I could sense the tension of their conversation so I really did not want to walk in on them. Anyway, I seem to remember carefully pulling the door open a little more and putting my head around it.'

'What did you see?' asked Florita.

Christy was still speaking quietly. She looked at their attentive faces before continuing.

'Papa was sitting motionless on the sofa staring at Mama who was standing in the middle of the room above him, berating him. In her hand was something in a plastic, carrier bag. Some kind of uniform I guess. Anyway Mama was disgusted by what she held in her hand. That much I could see. She continued to quietly berate Papa. I remember her words almost as if she was in the room speaking now, *'You stay out all night with your 'boyfriends' in your strange clubs leaving me behind to look after your daughters and to cover up for you if there are any questions. You always blame it on being a result of the pressures of being a politician, a public figure. I don't believe that and I never have. You have always lied to me Tomeu and you always will. I still love you my god, I don't know why, yes I do, I*

265

have had a life free from poverty, yes, you rescued me from that, and I have five gorgeous children. What I will not stand for Tomeu is you bringing these things,' she threw the carrier bag at Papa, *'Into my home. Never do it again!'* Mama then stomped away into the kitchen. I went back to bed and pretended to be asleep.'

Christy paused for breath. The other three were stunned, unable to speak. Christy had provided an image of their parents none of the sisters had ever considered before. It took awhile, but eventually Albert said what the others were thinking.

'So he actually was a homosexual, he was living a lie all this time?'

Florita and Montse nodded, deep down they were not that shocked by Christy's words. When Albert had mentioned it earlier they had been defensive, but they were both surprisingly aware of the possibility.

'His love for Alfonso Carboner was probably his driving force for the Millenarium thing, not religion after all,' added Albert. Then with a concerned and urgent look on his face he said, 'We need Ferran's help to find them.'

Reason to Believe

43

'You must have the wrong information Jesus! How can he have been released?' shouted an exasperated Ferran into his mobile as he sat up alert in the passenger seat of the police Seat being driven by his partner Maria.

He listened.

'OK! Get to the Gran Via bureau and check it out. Who released him and why?'

As he finished speaking he slammed his phone shut.

'What?' asked a concerned Maria, eager for information.

Ferran frowned and gasped, 'Xavi has been released.'

'What!'

'That was Jesus. He had a call from an inspector at the station, a friend who was surprised by the action and thought he ought to know. Jesus said that his friend revealed that some politician arrived with a legal document demanding Xavi's release and threatening to take the department to court for wrongful arrest and unlawful imprisonment.'

'So they gave in and just let him go?' said a disgruntled Maria.

'As always,' replied an intensely annoyed Ferran.

The two detectives sat in silence for a few minutes focussed on the road ahead, thinking. Then Maria spoke.

'That must mean that there is another person linked to the Creed, unless it was Ramon. There is no way the mad priest Jordi could pretend to be a politician.'

'I am sure the Creed has many sleeping partners who are loosely involved. It is like a secret society. There will be plenty of 'Brothers' in the upper echelons of our society,' mused Ferran.

Then he thought a little more.

'However, I really don't think it would be Ramon. He is just a chemist. You must be right, Xavi has obviously pulled a few strings.'

Another period of silence followed. Within a few minutes they arrived at the apartment building Victor had told the police about before he had been killed in his cell. An

Reason to Believe

alert local police unit had just sealed off the area outside the apartment building. Ferran and Maria dashed into the building and raced up the stairs to the second floor ignoring the lift. The door to the apartment was ajar. They both unholstered their handguns and held them steadily in front of them. Ferran signalled, 'Go!' with his eyes and then they both rushed into the apartment. There was no one there. They quickly searched the rooms to the new apartment before both returning to the main living room. There, on two large dining tables, were a whole host of chemical apparatus. Two Bunsen burners were still burning and a grey liquid was gurgling through a series of glass tubes. The two detectives looked at the apparatus confused and worried.

'Is this the virus or the antidote? Get forensics here quick,' Ferran instructed Maria who was already on her phone to central command. Ferran looked around the room searching for anything that was out of place or unusual that might give them a lead. He spotted blood on the hard tiled floor and walked over to take a closer look. Maria finished her call and joined him. Both of them crouched around the blood that had been dripped and then smudged across the floor. They both looked away from the blood at the rest of he room.

'Nothing much here at first sight,' commented Ferran.

Steve Kenning

'Forensics might find something more,' added Maria, before continuing, 'Where to now?'

Ferran tried to stand up but had to do so slowly and with a little pain, 'Oh my old knees!' he complained. Maria, ten years younger than her partner in the force and in life, sprang up onto her feet and smiled mockingly at Ferran.

'Come on old man, let me help you,' she said reaching out to support him. A she pulled his arm she noticed something out of the corner of her eye.

'Look!' she pointed with her right arm outstretched in the direction of the hallway.

'What?' replied Ferran, alerted but with no idea what he was looking for.

'Behind the door,' Maria said as she moved towards it. She closed the door to the hallway and lifted off a smart plain black jacket from the hook behind the door. Ferran was now with her and between them they searched the pockets, pulling a range of things out from paper, matches, money and plastic cards. There was a lot of small stuff in the pockets of the jacket. They laid it all out on the floor. The two detectives knelt on the floor and sifted through the contents of the pockets. Two things interested them. A small ring bound pocket book and a large key. Maria leafed through the pocket book.

'Anything?' asked Ferran hopefully.

Reason to Believe

'Nothing, it's empty,' said Maria as she turned the pages over one by one, 'Wait, here! There are two numbers. They look like city telephone numbers not mobiles, they start with 903,' she said with a sense of rising excitement evident in her voice.

'Well let's try them. We've got this key as well. Looks like it belongs to something old,' added Ferran, 'I think we are going to find our answers in the old city, the Ciutat Vella,' he remarked instinctively.

Maria was back on her phone as the two detectives raced down the stairs of the new apartment block. Outside Ferran gave instructions to the two police officers on guard. Maria was investigating the owners of the two phone numbers she had found in the pocket book.

This time Ferran took the drivers seat and Maria, still with the phone glued to her ear, sat in the passenger seat. Ferran roared the engine and received a disapproving look on the face of Maria. The car roared away from the apartment on the outskirts of the city and headed for the Ronda del Dalt, the road that feeds the northern suburbs of the city. As they drove along the busy highway Maria scribbled on a piece of paper resting on her knees. After several minutes she put her mobile away into her inside jacket pocket.

'Anything?' asked Ferran.

'Quite interesting,' replied Maria with a look of gentle excitement on her face.

'It seems that the numbers belong to Senor Tomeu Moncada. Both numbers are at the same address in the Ciutat Vella.'

'Where exactly?' questioned Ferran suspiciously.

'Calle Flassanders, number 8,' replied Maria.

Ferran looked ahead and rammed the car gear stick downwards into fourth gear before accelerating rapidly up a slope and past two slow moving vehicles.

'Let's go have a look!' smiled Ferran accelerating even harder.

Reason to Believe

44

'For the Lord I will give my soul. For the Lord I will give my soul,' ranted Father Jordi repetitively in a sullen voice. He looked out of reality in a world completely of his own. Brother Xavi looked at him with concern etched all over his face.

'Father Jordi!' Brother Xavi rasped eventually. It had an effect. Father Jordi was silent and stopped rocking backwards and forwards. He simply stood still hands clasped, looking ahead of him into a vacant space.

Ramon was shivering. He was thin and wiry and he had no jacket. The three of them were stood inside a small alleyway near to the Santa Maria del Mar church, trying to avoid both the heavy autumn rain and being seen.

Steve Kenning

'What now?' asked a nervous, cold, Ramon.

Xavi looked at him. He still retained an air of authority and assuredness, despite his brief uncomfortable spell in a cell. Staring at the younger man he simply replied, 'Calm your self my Brother. Now is the time. We simply need to wait for our leader.'

Ramon looked confused.

'Our leader? Alfonso Carboner?'

Father Jordi had been listening, despite appearing to be in a state of trance, he too had taken in the conversation. He turned towards the other two and listened for Xavi's response.

'Not Alfonso Carboner, but part of his inspiration and his chief disciple,' smiled Xavi.

'Who is that?' questioned a frustrated Ramon. Jordi continued to listen.

Xavi smiled confidently to himself.

'You just need to wait. It will not be long and then our mission will be complete.'

That seemed to satisfy Ramon slightly, as he just leant against the stone wall and shivered within himself. Father Jordi adopted a cross-legged position deep in a dark corner of the alley and meditated quietly. Xavi simply strolled from side to side of the alleyway thinking openly.

After twenty minutes or more of cold silence, his mobile rang baroquely.

Reason to Believe

'Yes! Yes! We are ready. Yes we will,' he responded.

Then he looked at the other two and raised his arm before moving away out of the alley.

'Come, quickly.'

45

As Albert, his wife and her two sisters hurried out of the James I metro station on Via Laietana and headed along Calle Argentera, Florita dialled a recently well-used number on her mobile.

'Ferran! Florita,' she said, listened for a reply before responding, 'Yes, good. Where are you?'

She listened carefully to the detectives reply.

'So are we. Where are you heading? Flassenders?' she stated before going quiet again as she let Ferran speak.

'No, Albert has a theory. We are heading for Calle Moncada. The palace, you know the one with the secret room.'

Reason to Believe

Florita heard his final words and said goodbye.

'Why Flassenders?' asked Albert as they strode purposefully along the crowded street.

'I think they traced a telephone number,' replied Florita.

Albert shrugged his shoulders.

Montse was annoyed by this action, 'Why are you so sure Albert you know where we need to go? You are being very arrogant, Ferran may have another lead,' she chastised.

Albert was a little surprised by this outburst.

'I'm sorry Montse, but it just came to me. I now I am right. I can't explain it, but I have a feeling that we are going to resolve this situation one way or another at the Palau dels Marquesos de Llio. I think Ferran is heading in the wrong direction,' he said with confidence.

Montse looked at her husband, grabbed hold of his hand and put her head to his cheek in forgiveness. The four of them carried on walking dodging the pools of water that lay on the smooth paved street.

46

Maria held on to the dashboard of the white Seat with her arms outstretched as the battered car screeched to a halt on Passeig de Picasso, just opposite an entrance to the entrancing Parc de Ciutadella. Maria stumbled out of the car, grateful to still be alive. It wasn't the time to criticise her partner's eccentric and excessive driving skills. She looked across at him as he got out the car. He was centred and focussed. Determined and driven, Ferran marched off towards the old city.

The habitual coachload of Japanese tourists delayed the two of them slightly on Calle Commercial. Ferran became massively frustrated as his six foot five inch frame got tangled up amongst several five foot nothing inch japanese

Reason to Believe

tourists. He tried to remain calm as he ploughed a gentle escape route. Eventually Ferran and Maria reached Passeig del Born where they enjoyed the space and some rare autumn sunshine. As they expanded their strides in the openness of the Passeig, the sun disappeared behind some large clouds and the rain began to fall intensively. Maria and Ferran hurried into the narrow streets of the old city.

'OK, where to now?' asked Maria as she followed Ferran closely into a dead end alley.

He looked at her with the rain pummelling his long black hair. He thought for a moment before replying.

'I thought I knew but now I'm not sure.'

They stopped walking and sheltered from the intense rain in a stone doorway. Maria huddle next to her detective partner

'What now? I thought you had a lead?'

'I did,' replied Ferran, 'But then I realised that the phone number addresses were no more than diversions. I really don't know exactly what we are looking for anymore. I wonder if Florita has discovered anything?' queried Ferran in exasperation.

With that comment he leant against the stone wall to a narrow doorway on the far edge of the Passeig del Born and touched the screen of his iphone.

'Florita, what have you and your family discovered?'

There was a pause as he waited for a reply.

'Not a great deal. We are determined to stay in the city though,' replied his former lover.

'Where are you now?' asked Ferran.

'We are in the Ciutat Vella,' replied Florita.

'Oh, so are we,' answered Ferran.

'So what lead have you?' asked Florita.

'Unfortunately nothing I feel, we are chasing shadows.'

'Well, I'm sure that we are faring any better than you Will,' she paused thoughtfully for a few seconds, 'But Albert seems to think he has a hunch and so we're heading down Corders, moving quite quickly towards the Palau dels Marquesos de Llio,' informed Florita.

Ferran thought about her words as he and Maria trudged along Princesca in the heavy rain.

'Yes! I think your brother-in-law might be right. It must be the place. Why didn't I think of it before?' reacted Ferran.

'Come on Maria, we need to get to Caller Moncada,' said Ferran initially forgetting about Florita on the other end of his mobile call. Then he remembered.

'We are coming to join you. Wait for us outside the Palace,' ordered Ferran.

Reason to Believe

47

A small group of people huddled in the growing gloom just out of the torrential rain under the archway to the Palau dels Marquesos de Llio. Opposite them, along the tall, narrow man-made canyon created by the grand palaces of Calle Moncada, was the perennial queue for the Picasso Museum. Albert looked at the tourist queue, made up of assorted different nationalities. He couldn't help thinking that there was much more for them to see in his beloved Ciutat Vella than the disappointing Museo de Picasso.

'Where are they?' questioned Montse, stamping up and down to keep warm. She was only wearing a thin blue sweater and was soaked through to the skin. Albert put his arm around his wife to give her some warmth. Florita looked impatiently down the narrow street.

'He said they were just coming onto Princesca. They can't be far away.'

At that moment Ferran and Maria appeared from behind a crowd of Japanese tourists.

'Oh, thanks for waiting for us,' uttered Ferran, 'let's go inside shall we?'

The six of them moved quickly into the palace courtyard before moving up the grand stone stairway towards the solid oak door that provided an access into the grand building. Water ran down the ancient stone walls, despite being inside the covered courtyard. The unusually heavy spell of rain was penetrating everywhere in this city desperately ill prepared for rain. Ferran, with his huge six foot five frame, eat up the stairs two at a time, with Maria, fit and nimbly keeping pace with him albeit taking one step at a time. Albert and the sisters struggled up the large stone stairs behind the two detectives.

Ferran didn't wait for anyone as he stormed to the top of the stairway. At the huge oak doorway he reached for the iron door handle and pushed the door open. Within a few seconds the small group were all stood within a large wood floored room that was remarkably warm and dry. Christy, the last in, gently closed the door. As they shuffled around

Reason to Believe

the well-furnished grand old room gradually warming up, they all searched for another exit.

After several minutes Ferran asked the question the rest were thinking.

'Come on Albert. You were transported to a lower room from this place. Where were you standing, surely you can remember?'

Albert said nothing but was clearly thinking. The others continued to search for another door or exit. Albert wandered over to the corner of the room furthest from the door they had entered the room from. He pushed at the stones on the wall whilst he desperately tried to recall his and Senor Moncada's actions in that room several days ago. He remembered taking in the ancient beauty of the room but not particularly listening to or watching his father in law. As Albert stood deep in thought in the far corner Ferran wandered over to him.

'OK Albert, where were you standing? There?' he pointed. Albert thought for a second and then moved slowly to the right and he realised he had been in exactly that same position once before.

'I was here, I remember now. Senor Moncada was standing there just to your right Ferran,' he pointed, 'I think, yes I remember now, he did, he put his hand on that wooden dado rail thing,' he continued as he gestured towards a gold painted, wooden patterned decoration that ran across the wall at a position just above mid-height. Ferran turned towards the wall and ran his fingers along the top of the wooden rail. Nothing. He stooped down a little and then looked underneath the rail before carefully running his fingers along the full length of the rail. Half way along he stopped his hand.

'There is something here,' he said as he stopped in order to identify exactly what it was his fingers had found. Albert joined him and stared at the golden rail. They could see nothing, although Ferran's fingers felt something on the rail. He pressed the extrusion but nothing happened. Ferran let go of the rail and stood up in frustration. Albert moved forward and ran his fingers underneath the rail. He stopped when he felt the extrusion. He stood up straight, with his back to the wall and tried to take the position he thought his father in law had taken. He rested his hand on the rail above the extrusion. For a few minutes he stood there with his hand firmly pressing the extrusion. He looked at Ferran.

'It will be something very clever,' he said.

'What do you mean?' replied the detective.

'They know or knew what they were doing. We know there is a way into the secret room but it will not be a simple switch that opens it up. Your forensic team couldn't find it. We have to take our time.'

Albert kept his hand on the wooden rail. The three sisters and Maria completed their surveyance of the room.

Reason to Believe

They joined Albert and Ferran in the far corner. As Albert fixed himself against the wall they crowded around him, all keen to resolve the puzzle.

'I think it is definitely something around here,' said Albert glancing from side to side.

He was right. Without warning the floor beneath Ferran disappeared. A slab of rock about a metre square covered in a Persian rug suddenly dropped from view. Ferran was standing directly above it and disappeared with it. His shocked, surprised expression brought an involuntary and inappropriate giggle from Christy. Within two seconds the stone was back in place minus Ferran.

They all stared at the place Ferran had stood a few seconds ago.

'Quick! Let's Go. Get on that slab,' ordered Montse. The three sisters and Maria jumped on, huddling together. Maria was particularly agitated. She wanted to be with her partner, to support him. They stared at Albert. Within a few seconds the stone slab dropped. Several minutes later Albert had joined the rest of the group in the secret room.

It was dim in the small, lower room. Light emitted from several candle lights around the low stone walled room. Albert knew this was the same room in which he had seen the orb. However, there was no sight of it now, although that particular experience was etched on his mind.

Steve Kenning

'It was just there,' he said as he pointed to the stone wall that ran along the length of the room.

The others said nothing. There was nothing to see. Albert felt embarrassed as if everyone thought he was making it all up. Ferran sensed his mood and placed a re-assuring hand on Albert's shoulder.

'Don't worry Albert, we know you saw something, remember forensics found some chemical evidence here.'

'OK. Where now?' said Maria thinking and looking around the strange little room. She was trying to move things on and find a lead but she knew Ferran would be well ahead of her in his thinking.

'Over here,' commanded Ferran as if he had read Maria's mind in that instant. He was standing on the far side of the room just underneath one of the candle lights.

'There is a door here,' he informed the others, 'Shall we go through?' he stated, not wanting or expecting an answer. The room was particularly dim in that section and it was hard to see anything on the roughly hewn stone wall. There was a slight outline of a door no more than five feet tall barely visible in the rock. Ferran had only noticed it by running his hands across the stone. Almost by accident he had found a raised euro sized stone that turned in on it self when touched and which acted as a small door handle.

Reason to Believe

'Maria, back me up,' he said as he took his gun from his shoulder holster. Maria did likewise and hurried over to his side. The others held back, slightly involuntarily.

48

There was a real air of tension as Maria put her index finger into the small stone cavity. She pulled on the edge of the stone and the door sprung open into the room they were standing in. Ferran ducked low and raced through the open door into the open space that lay behind. The anticlimax was evident on his face, as, within moments, he turned back disdainly informing the others of what was behind the door.

'A long, high ceilinged, stone corridor,' he sighed, 'We need to do it all again Maria. Come on.'

Ferran signalled to Maria to follow him down the long narrow corridor. There was a light at the far end of the corridor some twenty metres away so they could see roughly where they were headed. Albert led the others after Maria.

Reason to Believe

Ferran hurried along, his leather soled, expensive designer shoes, clapping on the stone floor creating an echo that reverberated along the corridor. He slowed as the narrow stone walls that formed the sides of the corridor came to an end. Ahead of him was a square area that appeared to have no real purpose. The walls were painted yellow and a high mini gold chandelier type light illuminated the area. To Ferrans left were some stone steps that led underneath the floor he was standing on. The others grouped behind the detective all wondering what lay under their feet.

Ferran sensed something or somebody and he put his index finger to his lips to encourage them all to be quiet. Then he stepped as quietly as he could down the stone steps. The line of the six adults heading down the stairwell moved as quietly as they possibly could. The stairwell turned through two, ninety degree turns before opening into a large foyer with two heavy wood doorways facing them. They stopped and looked. Ferran and Maria were visibly trying to decide which door to open first. Ferran sensed the door on the left was the correct one and signalled his choice with a nod towards his partner. She agreed and returned the nod. They quickly moved over to the door. Maria grabbed the door handle and repeated her earlier action. The door swung open and Ferran, gun at the ready, dashed into a brightly lit room.

Steve Kenning

The detective flew into the room and took up an aggressive stance, gun ahead of him, grasped in both his hands, held at chest height. Maria shot into the room right behind him, with her gun also finely poised. The others followed close behind, nearly stumbling into Maria and Ferran who had come to a surprised halt as soon as they had entered the room. Ferran and Maria were speechless for a few seconds, whilst the sisters all let out a simultaneous involuntary gasp. In front of them was a man they had never expected to see again.

'Welcome Montse,' he paused and added almost as an afterthought, 'And you Christy and Florita.'

'What? You are dead!' spluttered a visibly shocked Montse forcing her way to the front of the small group in order to come face to face with her Papa.

Senor Moncada stood proudly in front of them all, his back to the stone wall of a large, well furnished room, hidden deep in the old palace. He wore his regular green suit and waistcoast with a smart matching tie and white shirt. He looked relaxed and extremely healthy, with a completely different pallor compared to their last view of his grey, lifeless body in the mortuary. Next to him stood Brother Xavi and Father Jordi. Both were standing, legs apart, hands clasped in front of them. They too looked relaxed, almost smug.

Senor Moncada moved a little towards the small group.

Reason to Believe

'I suppose you are wondering, 'Why?' and 'What happened? Are you not dead?'

Ferran was used to surprise and he was soon back in control of the situation and immediately took the lead in the conversation.

'Before that Tomeu Moncada I have to inform you that you are under arrest for suspected terrorist activities and complicity to murder. The same applies to you Jordi Pique and Xavi Bosch. You will be taken to the Gran Via headquarters of the Mossos where you will have plenty of time to tell your story. Ferran and Maria held their guns towards the three men. Senor Moncada smiled.

'Of course detective, but my girls will not be there during the course of your interviewing so please let me give them a short explanation,' he announced calmly.

Ferran glanced at Maria and responded by nodding her approval.

'Ok, but be quick,' rasped Ferran, keeping his gun firmly in the line of Senor Moncada. Maria was watching the other two.

'Firstly, can we sit down?' asked the old man.

'Stay where you are,' rasped Ferran moving his gun towards the father of Montse, Christy and Florita, who all gasped at the severity of this response.

Senor Moncada looked at the detective casually before giving his attention to his girls.

'OK. I am sorry for leading you all over the city. You Albert,' he pointed, 'In particular. I like you a great deal but I went way over the top with you. I am sorry, but I had to do it.'

He looked towards Montse, then Christy and Florita.

'My girls, I love you all, but Montse, you are the one. You are all I ever wanted I am sorry to say. You provided the perfect cover for my political life, I am so sorry, girls,' he said forlornly looking at Christy and Florita, 'but I only ever wanted one child. It was your mother who insisted in having more. You children provided her with the love I could never give her.'

He stopped and laughed gently to himself, 'How I ever managed to make five of you I will never know.'

'You loved Mama!' insisted Montse angrily towards her father.

Senor Moncada looked at his daughter sympathetically.

'Yes I loved her in the best way I could, but I didn't really love her. By now you must have discovered that all my life I have loved and betrothed myself to just one person, and that person was not your mother.'

'Alfonso Carboner,' said Albert.

'Correct. We were lovers for over thirty years. He was my mentor, my master and he gave me a reason to believe. I have never been particularly religious, I was simply captivated by the thinking, the words and actions of

Reason to Believe

Alfonso. He died too soon. We had this plan but to truly be successful and create a new Millenarium, we had to wait for the year 2000. It became very complicated as we realised we did not have the scientific skills to manufacture the type of virus we needed to create. We had to find scientists and induct them into the Creed. It all took time and time ran out for Alfonso.'

As he spoke calmly Ferran was quietly boiling up with anger inside. He erupted verbally and explosively.

'How can you stand there and talk so calmly about a plan to kill thousands, if not millions, of people. It would never of worked,' said an angry Ferran.

The old man turned towards Ferran and smiled. He then ignored the detective and looked once more at Montse.

'I had to get you out of the city as I really was not sure you would be saved by the antidote,' he paused, 'You see, you are not a true believer. I had to give you a chance.'

Florita, hurt by her father's words entered the conversation and reacted with some strong words.

'You are an arrogant and unthoughtful pig Papa, how could you do this, how could you say these things to us, how could you trick us?'

Senor Moncada looked straight at her coldly.

'I have a mission and nothing,' he paused, 'Nothing could get in its way. Unfortunately I just couldn't let Montse suffer. I made a mistake, but it makes no odds now.'

293

Steve Kenning

'You bastard, you terrible man,' screamed Florita racing towards her father aggressively.

Albert held her back and tried to calm things down by changing the topic of conversation.

'How did you fool us that you were dead?'

'Easy,' replied the old man, 'Trimorphiaconfurtaline, a chemical that relaxes your heart so much it appears that you are dead. The unfortunate Brother Victor developed it by mistake.'

At that point there appeared to be no more to be said. Florita and Christy were sobbing and the others were left staring at Senor Moncada with disbelief written on their faces. The room went quiet.

Ferran reasserted his authority.

'OK! Enough talk Senor Moncada. It is time to go.'

As he started to unclip his handcuffs from his belt the old man replied.

'Not quite detective.'

'What?' queried Ferran annoyed by the intonance of defiance in the old man's voice.

'At eight thirty two this evening the vernal equinox will occur in the clear night sky. This marks the exact moment of Fra Dolcino's death and marks the start of the new Millenarium. At this point we will release the virus into the drinking water supply of Barcelona.'

Reason to Believe

'I am sorry to disappoint you sir,' Ferran said sarcastically, 'But the three of you are coming with us. You can explain your grand plans to the Mossos and I am sure they will let you drink as much of Barcelona's drinking water as you like.'

Ferran and Maria moved towards the three men ready to handcuff them. As they did so there was a significant flash, followed by a large amount of white smoke. As the room quickly became engulfed with the sulphurous gas the detectives could see nothing. They all coughed and spluttered. In the windowless room it took several minutes for the smoke to clear enough for them to even see each other. Ten minutes of floundering around the room later, the smoke had cleared but the three old men had long gone.

'Oh for God's sake!' said Ferran, 'Fooled by an eighty year old!'

49

'It's six p.m, we've got two hours,' panicked Christy.

The three sisters appeared white and stunned, partly as a result of the shock from seeing the father they had thought was dead, alive in the flesh, but also as a result of the unpleasant words their father had subsequently used towards them.

'I can't believe that he is the same man I grew up with. Was all his warmth and love he emanated for all those years simply pretence?' added Florita in disbelief.

'I think he has always been a little disturbed. Think back. There have been quite a number of occasions when he acted irrationally. Maybe as we loved him we chose not to

Reason to Believe

recognise those moments of weakness,' said Montse thoughtfully.

'Thinking about it, he and Mama had separate beds,' revealed Christy.

'And they never kissed or embraced in our company,' continued Florita, 'We thought it was because they would be embarrassed in front of us.'

Whilst the sisters were talking and trying to justify their Papas actions, Albert, Ferran and Maria had been walking around the large rectangular room looking for a way out. The room was high ceilinged and lavishly decorated in green, yellow and gold. Curtains were draped across parts of the walls from ceiling to floor. Pictures and furniture flooded the opulent space. There were no windows and no walls. The three of them were looking behind the curtains and pictures trying to find an exit. Simultaneously they all stopped. As one, they started to search solely with their eyes for the missing door that would undoubtedly lead to their escape.

'I just can't understand it,' queried Albert with a little rising panic in his voice, 'We came in from there,' he said pointing to a blank wall, 'But the door is gone. It's as if it has just sealed up. What I want to know is how did they get out? I can't see any seals or edges to the door.'

Ferran growled. He was quickly losing his patience.

'I know this is a visual trick. It is not logical otherwise. We came in and so we can get out. Also, they got out somehow. Are you telling me that an eighty year old and his two seventy year old accomplishes are more intelligent than we are? No! I don't think so.'

Maria was the only calm person in the room. She brushed back her long black hair from around her ears and put her mobile to the side of her head.

'Jesus! Good. Are you outside the Palace? Yes?' she questioned, 'We are stuck inside somewhere, probably in the basement.'

She listened to her colleague, a young detective working for the Special Investigations Unit.

'Yes, we went up the stairway by the Museo d'Textil and then into the Palace. Then we went into the big room and down a stairwell, before heading along a corridor into this room. Now we can't find the door,' she replied, 'OK?'

Ferran smiled at her.

'You are my dream. You alerted Jesus before we came. Yes?'

'Of course, as you always tell me, you always need to have a back up plan. Did you not pass your detective exams Ferran?'

Several minutes later a door opened from within a blank wall and the detective, Jesus Montageau, appeared to the delight of them all.

'How on earth did they do that?' marvelled Albert, staring at the wall.

Reason to Believe

'We will find out at some point Albert, but first we need to find those dangerous idiots,' said Ferran.

The detective followed Jesus out of the doorway that eventually led them outside the Palace. The others followed without a word, sensing Ferran's urgency.

50

'What time is it?' growled Ferran.

'6.45 p.m,' replied Maria.

'Where is the main water pumping station for the city? Let's try there first of all. It must tell us the location on the internet. Jesus call the office and have someone look it up,' the tense detective instructed as the three detectives quickly marched along Calle Moncada as they headed towards their parked cars on Calle Comerc. Albert was close by, skipping along on their shoulders, whilst the three sisters were struggling to keep up with the fast pace along the congested pavements.

'I think they will go outside,' suggested Albert from behind them.

Reason to Believe

'What?' replied a confused Ferran, 'Why?'

Albert caught them up a little.

'They want to see the equinox? They will want to be outside as they start the process of killing the unbelievers.'

The detectives thought for a second.

'He's right,' said Maria.

'I agree,' added Jesus.

Ferran considered this view, not understanding Albert's logic.

'OK. Where will they go then?'

'To the nearest outdoor reservoir,' answered Albert.

'Where is that?' asked Ferran.

'The Sau,' replied Albert.

Before long the seven of them reached Calle Comerc and piled into two cars. Ferran's car squealed as it burst away into the early evening traffic, closely followed by Jesus. There was no time to lose.

51

As they sped along the city streets Jesus was fairly relaxed in his pursuit of Ferran's white Seat. Inside his car were Albert, Montse and Florita.

'I've been reading up about the kind of people you have been investigating,' conversed Jesus.

'What do you mean by the 'kind of people?'' asked Montse.

'Millinarianists,' replied Jesus.

'So,' commented an intrigued Montse, 'What did you find out?'

'Well I searched the internet and found a load of information.'

Reason to Believe

'You're real generation Y material aren't you?' said Florita disdainfully to the young detective.

'Maybe,' replied the dark haired, confident detective. He drove quickly and precisely. He had sharp facial features and a young lean figure. He loved his job and he revelled in the common knowledge that he was Ferran's protégé.

'Go on. What did you find out?' asked Albert sending a scolding look towards Florita.

'Well,' Jesus began, 'Millenarian groups generally believe that the current society and its rulers are corrupt or just simply wrong. A common view is that society will soon be destroyed by a powerful force. They feel this way as they generally feel oppressed and so only dramatic change will change the world. This change will be brought about, and survived, by a group of the most devout and dedicated. Most Millenarian groups believe that the disaster to come is worthwhile and inevitable as it will be followed by a new, purified world in which the true believers will be rewarded.'

'We know all this,' drawled Florita.

'Go on,' urged Albert, again dispatching an annoyed 'shut up' look towards Florita.

'You probably know this as well then, but I will tell you anyway,' Jesus paused, 'There are hundreds of these groups operating at any one time in the world in this century. The numbers increase during difficult economic times. Today's economic climate is perfect for them. Groups such as al-

Steve Kenning

Qaeda, Branch Davidians and the Heaven's Gate Cult....have you heard of them?'

The others nodded.

'Many of these millenarian groups have pacifist tendencies, but at times they nearly all resort to violence. In some cases, they simply withdraw from society and await the intervention of God or aliens.'

The all sat silent in thought.

'Scary,' said Montse after a few minutes contemplation.

'Sorry to change the subject but Ferrans car just went that way,' pointed Florita towards a street they had just past.

Without hesitation or, in the eyes of Montse, looking, Jesus swung the old Mercedes around in a double u-turn and within minutes, once again had Ferran in his sights.

Reason to Believe

52

Maria was sitting next to Ferran in the front of the white Seat. Christy was strapped into the back seat holding on for all she was worth, as Ferran pushed the car to its limit along the busy streets of the city.

'Shall I call for back up Will?' asked Maria.

Ferran was hunched forward over the steering wheel focussed solely on the road. He took a few seconds to reply.

'I don't think so,' he growled, 'What would we say? Three pensioners are threatening to poison the population of

Barcelona, send your anti-terrorist team?' He laughed mockingly but with a hint of frustration.

Maria nodded in agreement.

'The three of us, plus our compatriots, are going to have to deal with these senior terrorists,' Ferran continued.

The car left the outskirts of the city and joined the C25 autoroute and headed for the provincial town of Vic.

'Where are we going?' asked Christy.

Ferran did not reply at first. He held back but after a few minutes decided to share his thoughts.

'Albert was right. Your father and his friends are wanting some kind of validation for their beliefs. They want to see the equinox as a message from God that what they are doing is the right thing,' replied Ferran.

'But they are committed. They're fanatics. They know they are right,' argued Christy.

'Yes but they want God's thanks. They're looking for a third person affirmation from their Lord. Where better than in the mountains where they have a clear view of the wide open sky.'

'Where are we going?' repeated a mystified Christy.

Ferran smiled.

'To Barcelona's largest water supplying reservoir, the Sau,' he informed.

'Do you think the old men will be there?' she asked.

Reason to Believe

'I hope so, otherwise if they are true to their word then we have a problem,' Ferran said with a blank expression on his face.

53

The sun had long disappeared downwards beyond the horizon and now the car headlights created a swathe of light across the bare hillside. Maria and Christy were rolling from side to side as the car fired its way up the mountain track. A little way behind them the second car, the Mercedes, struggled to keep with the pace. The sky was bright with stars, and, way back behind them, thirty miles away in the distance they could see the lights of Barcelona. It was 7.30 p.m.

Ten minutes later they were there. The Seat skidded to a halt across the gravel track as Ferran slammed on the brakes. He jumped out of the car and stretched his aching

Reason to Believe

limbs. Maria and Christy followed. A minute later the blue Mercedes arrived too. All seven of them set off for the top of the dam without a word, it was 7.43 p.m.

The light was incredible. The car lights were switched off, replaced by an illumination created simply and naturally by a huge full moon and a sky abundant with stars. The night was beautiful. The seven occupants of the two cars struggled out of the vehicles and immediately each one of them was momentarily dumbstruck by the vastness of the sky and the surreal light illuminating them. The group were lit up as if they were under floodlights as they hurried across the huge concrete structure that was holding back millions of cubic litres of water. Like them, everything else in the region was easily visible and they instantly picked out two figures looking towards them from the far side of the dam. As they quickly closed the gap between the two fugures and themselves they easily identified them as Senor Moncada and Xavi Bosch. The two elderly men stood staring at the group rapidly approaching them. They were unmoved and unconcerned.

Senor Moncada was particularly relaxed, leaning against the concrete structure, smiling profusely.

'You escaped from that room much quicker than we thought. Perhaps you are more intelligent than we had calculated,' said Senor Moncada sneeringly, ignoring the eyes of his daughters. He simply focussed on Ferran. Close to they could all see that the old man was not quite as relaxed as he had at first seemed. Sweat was glistening on his forehead and Senor Moncada and Brother Xavi both had worried looks on their faces. Their self-satisfied smiles of earlier had gone.

'Where is the priest?' asked Ferran aggressively ignoring the smug opening comment.

The two men said nothing initially in response to the detective. Instead they looked at each other before looking back towards Ferran. United they looked at a specific point on the concrete wall, pointed and said, 'There!'

Father Jordi leapt up from behind the dam wall brandishing a knife in his right hand. He moved quickly and had the benefit off surprise. He slashed Ferran's chest and plunged his knife into Jesus's shoulder before either of them could react. A shot rang out. The priest staggered as he moved towards Maria then he tripped and fell over the low dam wall. He dropped several hundred feet before he hit the ground below. Maria stood there, legs astride, gun held directly in front of her face with both hands.

Ferran was stunned, but his wounds were only superficial. Jesus however, looked white as he held his hand on the deep wound. Christy leapt forward and applied rudimentary first aid using her scarf and tissues. She helped Jesus into a sitting position. Montse and Florita helped, but

Reason to Believe

it was obvious that he was going to be OK as the blood was simply seeping from the deep wound.

Within a few minutes the brief commotion was over and the small group recovered their composure. Jesus was sitting comfortably and Ferran realised that his wounds were little more than scratches. Together they turned back towards the two elderly men. The old men looked unmoved and expressionless.

Ferran, with his white shirt slashed open and splattered with blood, moved towards the two men.

'What are you hoping to achieve? There are two of you left, perhaps three. What kind of world do you hope to create? You have killed, you have destroyed your family Senor Moncada, and now you want to kill many innocent people. You decry the corruptness of society today but how corrupt are you? I ask you how corrupt are you?' he paused waiting for a response. Before the old man had time to respond he continued, 'I am disgusted by you,' ranted the detective.

The two old men said nothing. They stared in front of themselves into empty space totally ignoring the detective.

Albert stepped forward. He spoke quietly.

'Senor Moncada, Brother Xavi, I am surprised and disturbed by your actions. As you know I am a scholar of philosophy and, as a result, I have read a great deal about your religion,' he stopped speaking and shook his head in disbelief. Then he continued, 'I believe you have been blinded by your love for Alfonso Carboner. I say to you that it is your love for him, rather than your distaste for the failures of the modern world, that is driving you on and giving you your purpose.'

Albert paused and looked the two old men straight in the eyes. They were listening.

'If you start out with the wrong premise, you are bound to come to the wrong conclusion. All wrong thinking leads to wrong action. It is important that you as Christians know the truth, speak the truth, and defend the truth. The Gospel of John 8:32 tells us, "You shall know the truth and the truth shall make you free." This sounds good but has the wrong premise and inevitably the wrong conclusion,' informed Albert.

'Truth doesn't set one free. Only truth that you know intuitively does. Therein lays the battle. Most Christians do not know the truth intuitively. They merely repeat someone else's version of it. That is what you are doing, repeating Alfonso Carboners truth.'

Albert stopped speaking. He was really pushing at the beliefs of the two old men. He was challenging their belief. He looked around. Everyone, including the injured Jesus lying propped up on the ground, was captivated by the words of this man whose words were so powerful.

Reason to Believe

'Carry on Albert,' urged Montse aware of the impact of his tone and presence. He did as he was told.

'"If you tell a lie big enough and keep repeating it, people will eventually come to believe it." These are the words of Joseph Goebbels. Remember, truth is not relative, and it is not an opinion handed down by some judge, perhaps a judge such as Alfonso Carboner. Truth stands alone against the weathering of time. Jesus said in John 17:17 "Sanctify them through thy truth: thy word is truth."'

Albert could see that his last few words had left his audience slightly bemused.

'What I am saying is that you must know your own truth, not the truth told you by another. Listen to yourself. Take readings from your heart. Allow the moral voices inside your head to lead you to the right course of action. Clear your mind and do what you believe is right.'

That was all that needed to be said. He was appealing to the old men. Albert stopped speaking and a silence fell around the assorted company. It was 7.57 p.m. Time appeared to stand still. Jesus struggled to his feet with the help of Christy holding his patched up shoulder. The two other detectives, Albert and the three sisters all stood and stared at Senor Moncada and Brother Xavi. Xavi looked agitated and kept looking nervously towards his obvious superior Senor Moncada, who was giving nothing away with his expression. When he eventually spoke it was as if he was addressing a political assembly. He prepared himself before starting to speak.

'Albert, you surprise me, however not with your intellect and knowledge, but with your ability to transmit a sense of belief. When you were just speaking I felt myself believing your words and, I have to say, for the very first time, I have wondered if our mission is right.'

The old man looked towards Albert.

'Over there!'

He pointed to the bank of the reservoir near the end of the dam wall.

'There are twenty barrels of TX780 awaiting my instruction. I have the power in my hand to press a button to release a deadly virus into the water supply of that city over there,' he said as he pointed towards Barcelona. However, you have sown a slight seed of doubt in my mind. I still believe in the words of Alfonso Carboner with all my self, yet I will trust in the Lord. At exactly 8 p.m we will be sent a message in the sky from the Lord to guide us forwards on our mission. If we do not I will hand over the explosive device,' stated Senor Moncada.

It was now 7.59 p.m. Every one of them looked up at the bright, evening sky. There was silence. Ferran watched both men looking for a sign of the trigger. It was quite cold and both of the old men had their hands in their overcoat pockets. He could see the barrels and so he knew there were

Reason to Believe

serious so he couldn't take the risk of taking the wrong man out and allowing the other to detonate the virus. Should he leave them alone and see if the sky gave a message or should he take a risk? He was undecided. Maria caught his eye. He instinctively knew she was thinking what he was thinking. Their eyes worked together and suddenly he knew exactly what they had to do.

The sky started to light up even brighter so that it almost felt like daylight, something was happening and the time was 8 p.m. Not all the group would see the resultant natural phenomena. Instinctively, both Ferran and Maria fired a shot into the head of a man standing right in front of each of them. Senor Moncada and Brother Xavi dropped to the floor. Death was instant. As they lay in a combined crumpled mass on the ground the sky of the equinox performed miracles. It was spectacular. Lights filled the sky and changed colour repeatedly. Was this a sign that they had done the right thing and stopped the Dulcinian Utilitarian Creed or was it notice that there was another group of fanatical Millenarianists, somewhere else in the world that had just set the world on course for another Millenarium?

Steve Kenning

www.tiradorspress.co.uk